Becky and Chad and the Bugs in the Basement

Millie M.

Content Warnings

Beetles and spiders and worms, oh my!

Come along with Chad and Becky as they get frisky with the monstrous menagerie that lurks behind the crack in their basement wall.

Enthusiastically consensual, playfully horrific monster erotica.

Content warnings for taboo erotica featuring giant bugs, sibling incest, and cannibalism.

Contents

Chapter One

OUR STORY BEGINS A few days after Becky and Chad move into a new house.

The house wasn't really new, but it was new to them. In fact, the house had been there for almost two hundred years. It was built right into the side of the hill, which rose up to join the other hills framing the hollow that embraced the property. It was quiet and private and beautiful, and Chad and Becky both loved it.

The hollow was shaded by hardwood trees, and a creek ran down the nearby cliff-face before disappearing into the ground. Rich ground nurtured a full yard of green grass which got enough sunlight over the course of the day that Becky was sure that it would be bright enough to grow flowers in the Spring.

Truly, it was perfection.

The location was good, too. It was in the country, but close enough to town that Chad could comfortably commute to his job. And as far out as they were, it was still on the right side of the area supported by the local wireless company, so Becky was able to continue working from home.

The only concern they had was the crack in the basement wall—the old stone wall that backed against the hillside. The crack ran diagonally from the top left corner of the wall to the bottom right, and was wide enough for Chad to stick his arm through.

"I'm not afraid of creepy crawlies," Becky scoffed when their neighbor came by to greet them, and warn them about what lived under the mountains.

"Strange things lurk in the caves, the stories go back for generations," the neighbor had said, squinting at the house with dark eyes creased by wrinkles. "I've never seen anything myself, but you know. Better be careful."

Becky rolled her eyes, and Chad promised that they would be wary. The next weekend, Chad planned to go to Home Depot and pick up enough Quikrete to fill the crack right up. He admired Becky's bravery, but he didn't like the idea of creepy things crawling in from the caverns that twisted and turned through the ground beneath the hills. The neighbor's warnings had spooked him good.

Becky and Chad commemorated the purchase of their new house by fucking in the living room: doggy style, one of their many favorite positions. Becky was on her knees, leaning against the sofa with her legs spread wide and her ass in the air. She'd worn her favorite dress for their celebratory dinner, and Chad thought the dress looked very pretty with the skirt thrown up onto her back. He was on his knees, too, hard at work behind her, thrusting roughly enough to make her swear.

"Yeah, that's right," he muttered over the slick smack of skin on skin. "Take it all, take it—" Suddenly there was a clicky-clacking sound from the direction of the window, Chad paused his thrusting and his soliloquy to take a look.

"Hey babe," he said, squinting at the shadow under the window. "Is there something over there?"

Becky turned her head to follow his glance. "Yeah," she said, blinking through her tears of pleasure. "It looks like a... like a beetle?"

"Yeah, a beetle. But it's too big."

The beetle, which was shiny and black and at least two feet long, scuttled out a few inches into the light, giving them a better view.

Becky, drunk on beer and her own arousal, was remarkably cool about a giant beetle showing up in their living room to interrupt their lovemaking.

"Chad, I think it's watching us."

"Watching us? You mean it's watching us fuck?" He was incredulous.

"Yes, I think so. Hey beetle," she said, addressing the thing directly, and holding out her hand like she might to a curious kitten. "Do you like watching us fuck?"

To their surprise the thing clicked a few more times, scuttled sideways, and then stopped, facing them the entire time. Its antenna twitched.

"That's kind of hot," Becky murmured, pressing her cheek against the sofa cushion again. "Keep going, and see what happens."

It was weird—the sudden presence of the giant beetle, the interest in exhibitionism on the part of his girlfriend—but Becky was horny and Chad was so hard it was starting to hurt, so he thrust back into her

3

with a satisfying squelch. He reamed her, again and again, and when she finally started begging for it he reached a hand around, between her legs, and rubbed her clit. The sensation of her orgasm was familiar, muscles tightening and then a quick pulse accompanied by shouts of pleasure. The beetle—which had stood unmoving at the edge of shadow the entire time—scuttled just a few inches closer, and when Chad pulled out and spurted ropes of cum across her ass, grunting in satisfaction, the beetle scuttled again and made a chittering noise, like a cross between a cricket's chirp and a cat watching a bird play outside the window.

"You enjoy that?" Becky asked the thing, breathless, as Chad scooped up a finger of cum and sucked it off. "Come back tomorrow, there's a show every night." Chad offered Becky a finger, too, and she sucked it with a moan.

When they looked back at the window, the beetle was gone.

The beetle came back the next night, and it brought a friend. The friend looked like an ant, but thinner, and was even longer than the beetle. It had an extended abdomen that finished with a rounded point, the sight of which made Becky feel funny when she caught the two of them crouching in the corner of their bedroom, watching Chad eat her out.

"Baby," she moaned, tugging on his hair, "the beetle is back, and it brought another one."

Chad dragged his attention away from her pussy and followed her finger to where it pointed across the room.

"I need to get that Quikrete soon," Chad grumbled, but Becky demurred.

"I kind of like it, if you don't mind."

"You like the giant bugs watching us?"

Becky thought for a moment, chewing her bottom lip before answering. "Yeah, I do. I think it's hot."

The bugs scuttled closer to the bed, and the beetle chittered as it had the night before. Becky grinned.

"Yeah, you think it's hot too, don't you. Do you want to come up on the bed so you can see better?"

"Really?" Chad gazed up her body, meeting her eyes and looking annoyed, but she pouted at him.

"Please? It'll be fun."

Chad sighed. He was such a simp. "Okay, fine." The two of them scooted onto one side of the bed, leaving plenty of space for the two giant insects. "Come on, then," Chad said, waving them up, and very quickly the beetle and the ant climbed up the footboard and settled close to Becky's torso.

Chad got back to work, licking Becky's folds and sucking her clit, and she played with her nipples while she rolled her hips against his mouth. Once he was in the zone, concentrating on Becky's flavor and her little sounds of pleasure, he found it easy to ignore the bugs. He could tell that she liked having them there, though; even though he was trying to tease her, it only took a few minutes before she was getting close.

For her part, Becky was enjoying the sensation of Chad's tongue on her, and the pinch and pull of her fingers on her breasts. She, too, had noticed that the addition of the bugs to their bed did something to her. Something good. It was almost as good as when Chad's brother—

Suddenly, something moved her hands aside and started fondling her breasts.

Becky's eyes flew open and she looked down to discover that the ant had grasped her right breast with its mandibles and was massaging it, with surprising gentleness. The beetle was caressing her left breast between its first pair of legs.

It only took Becky a moment to decide that she was wholly in support of this particular endeavor. "Harder," she instructed all of them. "Harder!" All three of them, the man and the insects, obeyed her command, and within seconds she came so hard she saw stars.

Becky wasn't done.

"Chad, fuck me," she said, spreading her arms wide and stretching her arms above her head to give her new friends better access to her chest. Chad, who had been focused on his job between her legs, finally looked up and saw the insects on her breasts.

"Oh, fuck," he squeaked, nevertheless obeying her request and crawling up her body. "Doesn't that hurt?"

"Nope," she said, wriggling her ass. "It feels amazing, they are turning out to be quite helpful. Now put your dick in me, I want to come again."

Chad slid right in; she was as tight as always, but so wet that even though Chad was well above average in both girth and length, he slipped in easily.

"Oh, fuck," Becky moaned, taking pleasure in how her pussy stretched to take all of him, and in how the bugs massaged her breasts just right.

Chad was a bit shocked by how sexy Becky looked with the bugs on her, and although he wanted to make it last for both of them he could tell by the way the muscles in her pussy were beginning to clench that she was getting close again. He was just thinking about putting his thumb on her clit when the ant thing stretched out its middle leg closest to him and reached between her legs. The thing rubbed the back of the clawed end of its spindly black limb against her, and Becky cried out in pleasure as she came hard on Chad's dick. He tumbled right along with her pleasure.

"Oh, fuck," Becky moaned, as both creatures scuttled away from her and off the bed, apparently understanding that the fucking was over for the night. "Come back tomorrow night!" She called after them. "Bring more friends!"

"Fuck, yes," Chad moaned, lying down next to her and giving her a hug before reaching down to play with the cum leaking out of her pussy. "Those bugs are hot. Do you think they'd fuck you? Do you think they'd fuck *me*?"

"Oh, Chad." Becky said with a sleepy giggle. "I was just wondering the same thing."

Chapter Two

THE NEXT NIGHT THERE were four big bugs, which was more than Becky and Chad were expecting, but they weren't going to complain.

"Woah," Becky declared, partly because Chad's tongue was deep in her pussy and it felt really good, but also because one of the new bugs—a thing the same size as the ant but with shining compound eyes and shimmering green wings and a curved backside—was leaking fluid from its tapered end. Her pussy clenched in excitement at the thought of having it inside her. "I want to fuck that one."

Chad had heard the clatter of sharp feet on the hardwood and the familiar welcome chitter of the beetle, so he wasn't too surprised to lift his face from his girlfriend to see them there, lined up in a row along the wall.

"I think it wants to fuck you too, look at it dripping." As if on cue, the thing scuttled closer to the bed, leaving a trail of moisture to track its movement. Chad addressed it. "Hey, Wings, you wanna fuck my girl? Stick that thing in her and make her come hard?"

The thing—which would now forever be called Wings—trilled, a high, unearthly sound, and skittered to the end of the bed, then climbed up the footboard and perched directly above where Becky lay, her legs spread wide. Chad had already moved aside to make room for

8

the thing, his dick heavy and hard in his hand. The other bugs had followed their comrade, and flanked it along the top of the footboard.

"Okay," Chad said, breathing heavily, hardly believing that he was about to watch the love of his life fuck a giant insect from the caverns under their house. "You can do it, but on one condition."

Wings tilted its head towards him, clearly listening, but it was Becky who spoke.

"No eggs," she said with conviction, pointing her finger at all of them. Chad and Becky had discussed their limits, and this was one of them. "I will fuck any of you, however you want, but I'm not going to be an incubator for your babies."

"We have lots of towels," Chad added, pointing to a stack on the bedside table on the other side of Becky, "if you think you'll make a mess."

The four giant insects chittered amongst themselves for a moment and then the ant and beetle broke away and grabbed some towels with their mandibles, and with Chad's help used them to line the bed, placing a double layer under Becky's butt. In the meantime Becky stroked herself between her legs while she and Wings, still dripping copiously, made eyes at each other. The fourth one curled up on the bed and leered, but in a friendly way.

It was finally time. "Oh my God, I am so ready," Becky moaned, as Wings climbed onto her body and positioned its tapered end between her legs.

"No eggs," Chad whispered, as he helped the thing lower its body and angle itself so it could penetrate Becky's pussy.

Once Wings was inside Becky she thrust her hips up onto it once, twice, three times. Once Wings realized how much Becky could take, it

9

changed angles, giving her more of its body, pushing deeper and deeper. The ant and the beetle took their usual positions on her breasts, massaging and pinching them with their mandibles and feet, just as they had learned she liked it.

Chad sat back on his knees and watched as the thing on Becky thrust almost its entire abdomen into her. She sobbed, tears of pleasure flowing down her cheeks and dampening the pillow behind her head.

"Oh fuck, Chad, Wings, fuck me, fuck me so good, all the way," Becky babbled, copious amounts of fluid dripping down from where their bodies joined.

Chad was so into what they were doing that at first he didn't notice when the fourth bug clambered over and examined the precum beading on the tip of his dick.

"Oh yeah?" He said to it, dipping his finger in and offering it to the thing. "You want to try it?"

It did, and it reached out its head—really, just the end of its long, undulating body that contained the mouth—and took his entire finger into its gullet. It was moist and surprisingly warm in there, and the sensation made Chad's dick jump in his hand.

"It feels good in there," he said, pulling his finger out and wiping the sticky fluid off on his thigh. "You wanna suck me off? There's a lot more in there if you can get it out."

The thing chittered excitedly, but instead of just taking his dick it bumped against him.

"It wants you to move, babe," Becky moaned.

He moved to make room for the thing. It was the thickest, longest millipede Chad could even imagine, five feet long at least and it lay on its back in the middle of the bed, its dozens of little legs pointed at the ceiling.

Wings was still fucking Becky—hard, just the way Chad knew she liked it. "Does that feel good sweetheart?"

"Wings is a good fuck. Hey, Wings," she said, looking up at the bug, "will you fuck Chad next? He likes to be fucked in the ass and I would like to see that."

The thing chittered excitedly and reached one of its horned limbs between Becky's legs to rub her clit.

"I think that's a yes," Becky cried, anticipating a mind-blowing orgasm, but Chad was distracted. He'd figured out what their other new friend—Millie, he would call it—wanted him to do. He straddled Millie's body, and it scritched his balls and ass and the sensitive area between them with its little feet while it curled up its head and sucked his dick into its wet, generous mouth, taking as much as it could get.

"Oh, fuck," Chad moaned at the dual sensations, at the same time that Becky screamed and shuddered, grasping the headboard with white knuckles as Wings continued to fuck her through her orgasm.

But the thing had its own needs, and as soon as Becky began to relax it pulled out of her and, with a high-pitched whine, dropped a full clutch of white, gelatinous eggs, along with an impressive amount of white fluid, onto the waiting towels.

"Oh, Wings," Becky moaned, "that was so good for me, and you came too. Did you like it?"

The insect crawled up her chest and tenderly touched her cheeks with its antennae, then made its way over to where Chad was fucking Millie's mouth.

Becky thought Chad looked gorgeous: huge and naked, dark hair wild, abdominals tight, crouched over a giant millipede that appeared to be attempting to suck his soul out through his dick.

"That's a good look for you," she murmured, and reached out to trace her fingers along some of the bug's legs.

"I'm calling it Millie," he breathed out between grunts, "and it's good at sucking dick."

"Well lean forward, babe," Becky murmured as the winged insect climbed onto his back. "Wings is an excellent fuck and its dripping again already, if you want it."

Chad did want it, he wanted to come sandwiched between these amazing creatures, so with Millie's assistance he leaned forward and spread his legs wide, so both of them could have access to his body. He cried out as Wings's tapered end breached his asshole, but it was gentle and very wet, and soon it was thrusting several inches in.

Becky was so absorbed by the sight and sound and scent of her boyfriend fucking the bugs that she hadn't been paying attention to the beetle and the ant, their original friends and playmates that had come in through the crack in the basement. They'd been helpful again, disposing of the eggs, but they were back for more.

Becky eyed the backend of the ant, which was also starting to drip, a clear liquid that made Becky's mouth water.

"I see that," Becky said, biting her bottom lip. "You've been so good, both of you. How do you want to fuck me? You can do it however you want."

The two of them chittered together for a moment, and then moved down to her hips. The ant pushed against her knee, and she bent it up at the same time the beetle climbed on top of her and turned to face her, backing up until it was between her legs.

"Oooo, Chad!" Becky squealed, "they're going to DP me!"

Chad was still riding with Millie and Wings; they had apparently figured out how to give him just enough stimulation to keep him on the edge. He couldn't speak but did open his eyes to look over at Becky and the others.

"Watch this," she said. The ant eased its tapered end, now thoroughly slimy, into her asshole, and the beetle extended something from its underside—something soft but surprisingly thick and long—and pressed it into her pussy. Once it was inside her it thickened and thinned rather than thrusting in and out. The combined sensation of the two insects, one in her ass and the other in her pussy, was exquisite, and Becky keened and moaned and rolled her hips along with their movements. As Wings and Millie did with Chad, the ant and beetle appeared to be working together to bring Becky peak pleasure.

Becky's rational brain was almost completely overwhelmed, but she did realize before long that the thickening and thinning sensation of the beetle was it moving one of its eggs up and down the tube inside her.

"No eggs," she reminded them. The beetle paused and chittered, offended at the suggestion they might forget.

"I'm sorry to offend," she moaned, "just wanted to make sure."

The beetle accepted her apology, and brought one of its feet to her clit to let her know.

Apparently the bugs thought Chad had been waiting long enough; with just a touch more effort on the part of Wings and Millie, Chad came with a cry and a rush of tears; he sobbed as Millie sucked down his cum and Wings pulled out of his ass and climbed up his back to embrace him around his shoulders, depositing another clutch of eggs down his back and onto Millie's long belly.

The sight of Chad crying with eggs dripping down him pushed Becky over the edge, and she came again with a shout, her muscles squeezing around both the ant and the beetle. They held out as long as they could, but first one and then the other pulled out, more eggs and fluid dousing both Becky and the bed and filling the room with a sharp, earthy scent.

Becky and Chad found each other and cuddled, kissing while the bugs ate the eggs and sucked up the fluid. When the ant tried to pull one of the towels, Becky held her hand out.

"Please don't, we'll clean up the rest," she insisted. "Thank you so much for tonight. I hope it was good for you, too."

The giant insects all chittered together happily, and Chad laughed.

"That's great! See you again soon!"

"Bring more friends!" Becky called after them as they skittered out the door and down the basement stairs.

"That was amazing," Chad declared.

"It was. I'm so glad we bought this house and not the one in town."

"Oh, me too. Can you imagine trying to do something like this with those neighbors?"

Becky laughed too. "Not at all. These neighbors are much better.

"Maybe next time," she added thoughtfully, "they'll bring a spider."

Chapter Three

CHAD WAS OUT OF town for a few days, and Becky was excited.

She'd miss him, of course, but missing him was part of the charm. It meant she'd be very happy to see him when he returned home.

There was another reason for Becky to be excited, though. This would be the first time Becky had been home alone since they'd moved into their new house and made their new friends, and she was eager to have them all to herself.

There was, of course, no guarantee that anything would happen. The bugs didn't visit every night, and they didn't seem to have a schedule. They just came up whenever they were in the mood. Chad had explained to the bugs that he would be away, and that he was hoping they would be good to Becky while he was gone, but there was no guarantee that they understood what he was saying. They seemed to communicate pretty well during sex—their "no eggs" rule was clearly understood and always followed, and general consent seemed easy to understand—but they weren't sure how well more advanced ideas would get across.

The first night of Chad's absence there were no visitors. Becky was a little disappointed; she'd worked herself up quite a bit during the day, imagining what might happen, who might come to call and what they might do to her, but her handy vibrator coupled with a call with Chad was enjoyable if not entirely satisfying.

The second night the beetle and ant came to call. Becky felt a little bad that they didn't have names for them, although Becky now understood that unlike Millie and Wings, who were unique, there were actually several ants and several beetles, all of whom looked and acted exactly the same as far as Becky could tell. So she didn't feel that bad. In any case, beetle and ant came the second night and ant fucked her while beetle played with her clit, and she had a nice orgasm but only one, and ant hadn't even deposited eggs afterwards which she had to admit was a little disappointing.

The fourth night, Becky was alone when she went to sleep, no sign of anyone, and she thought it was going to be another lonely night with only her vibrator and a conversation with the distant Chad to keep her company. She was thus quite surprised when a creak and the click clack of multiple hard feet on the hardwood floor awoke her well after midnight. She flicked on her bedside lamp, and gasped at the sight that greeted her.

All the bugs were there—she had met many over the weeks they'd been living in the house and fucking the bugs, but she had never seen more than a few at a time, and handn't imagined how they might look all together. She was shocked to discover that there were even more than she could have imagined. There were dozens of them, worms and ants and bees, wasps and beetles and millipedes and so many others. They lined the floor and piled in the corners and crawled up the walls. Rather than frightening her, the sight of them and their sour, earthy scent made her mouth water and warmth pool in her tummy.

There were so many of them, and they were there for her.

As she sat up in bed, several of them crawled up on the bed and proceeded to pull the pillows and blankets down and lay them out in the only open space left in the room, the floor at the foot of the bed. The pillows they piled on one end and they laid out the blankets to form a pallet, warm and soft over the chilly hardness of the floor.

Wings perched on the footboard and chittered at her encouragingly, gesturing to the area on the floor with its antennae. Becky followed its direction, crawling to the end of the bed and gingerly climbing down to lay herself out on the ground, her head on the pillows. The bugs rearranged themselves, some of them crawling up onto the bed, but all of them staying where they should have a good view.

Voyeurism, then. The bugs sometimes like to watch, and Becky was more than happy to be watched, especially if it meant getting to fuck Wings. Wings was a good fuck, and they had been doing it enough that it could make Becky come without her even touching her clit. Not even Chad could do that.

Becky laid down, naked, and pulled her knees up to make space for Wings. But Wings was still perched on the footboard, and the other bugs were just sitting there, watching her, and as the seconds ticked past she was unsure of what exactly she was supposed to be doing.

But then there was a new sound in the house, more steps on the stairs—heavy and light together, lots and lots and lots of steps, and the bugs by the door moved aside to form a path to where Becky lay on the floor.

The path filled with a silver wave that flowed in from the hallway, and it wasn't until Becky pushed herself up on her elbow that she understood that the silver wave was hundreds—thousands, perhaps—of spiders. And not large spiders, but normal sized ones.

Becky was not normally a fan of spiders; they move strangely, quickly, and they have too many eyes. They're just plain creepy. But these were spiders from under the house, which made them her spiders, so instead of disgust she was filled with curiosity. What were the spiders going to do to her? She was a bit surprised to find that she wanted to feel them crawling on her skin, and she was disappointed when they didn't come to her; instead they moved past her, and took position on the wall across from her, where the other, large bugs had moved aside to make room for them. Everyone chittered excitedly, but when the heavy steps entered, the room became silent.

Into the room crept the largest spider Becky had ever seen, had ever imagined. She had a small head and a large, fat body that ended in a long protrusion with a rounded tip.It dripped a thick fluid onto the ground behind her. Her legs were long and strong, they extended above her body and then bent down, ending in claws that scraped against the floor as she crawled through the door.

Becky eyed the claws, and the long legs, and the dripping backside, and she was more excited than she had been in quite a while. This giant spider was here to fuck her, and all the other bugs were going to watch. Becky already knew it was going to be amazing.

She laid back down, and the spider—whom Becky had decided to call Elshob because such an amazing monster deserved a name that referred to the best giant spider ever but wasn't close enough to encourage legal action—creeped in beside her. The other bugs filled in the space. They were so excited they were practically vibrating, their movement and slight chittering filling the small space of the bedroom.

Slowly, carefully, the spider climbed on top of Becky. Elshob encouraged Becky to hold her arms above her head, and she held each of Becky's wrists against the floor in the claws at the end of her front legs. Her second set of legs she placed on either side of Becky's torso, and her third set she used to push Becky's knees apart and hold them steady. The claws on her back legs clapped Becky's ankles, which she then pushed Becky's legs even further apart. Elshob's body—black, bulbous, dripping—rested in the air just above the apex of Becky's thighs.

When they were settled the giant arachnid held Becky, without moving, and gazed down into her face. At least Becky supposed she was gazing; it was a bit hard to tell with so many eyes. But she felt regarded, and the part of her that loved it when Chad called her a *good girl* hoped the spider would find her satisfactory.

Becky was so hot, so wet and so ready. She needed to get fucked soon or she was going to cry. A whimper escaped her throat, and finally Elshob moved, not down, but she shifted up, and with a joyful-sounding chitter a number of bugs scuttled out from the gathering, passing under the spider and up onto Becky's body.

It was two beetles and an ant, and Becky said hello to all of them as they got into position. Each beetle claimed a breast, and together they massaged her soft tissue with their legs and plucked her nipples with their mandibles as the ant slowly eased its round, pointed backside into Becky's pussy. She couldn't move, Elshob was holding her too tight, so she was forced to lie back and take it.

She did, and it was so good, but without pressure on her clit it wasn't enough to come.

"Please, Elshob," she moaned, after a few minutes. "Please, this is so good but I need more."

Elshob chittered—the first time Becky had heard her make a sound. It was deep and loud and otherworldly, and it made Becky shudder with pleasure. But instead of redoubling their efforts, or touching her clit, the beetles crawled away, and the ant pulled out of her.

Becky sobbed, and pushed against Elshob's legs, but she still couldn't move. Another group of bugs came forward. This time it was a group of millipedes, not as large as Chad's Millie but still much larger than normal millipedes. As before, two of them climbed up her body and another one crawled between her legs, and with some trilled direction from Elshob they started to work on her. Their legs were stickly and delicate and they felt so very good against Becky's skin, tickling her nipples and pricking between her legs, up and around her inner and outer lips and into her ass, but it still wasn't enough. Becky tried desperately to press harder against them, to shift her body to help direct them where they needed to be, but the massive spider was too strong and steady and she couldn't move at all. Within minutes she was sobbing harder, crying out in frustrated pleasure.

With a chirp from Elshob, the millipedes ceased their movements, and quickly crawled away.

Wings was there next, not on her but next to her head. It chittered as though concerned, and Becky smiled at it through her tears.

"Yes, Wings, I like it. It's hard but I don't want to stop." She looked up at Elshob, the spider's multiple eyes shining purple and green and reflecting dozens of Beckies back at her. "Don't stop, Elshob, please. Please, I'll be good, please don't stop."

Seemingly satisfied, Wings retreated and another group of bugs came forward. Becky closed her eyes and didn't even register exactly what they were. Moths or butterflies, maybe; something with soft

20

wings and antennae paired with something that penetrated her, very stiff with a pronounced knob on the end. By this point all she could do was lie back and take it, the bugs pushing her body so close to orgasm she could taste it, but just not taking her all the way there.

This happened several more times over the next hour; Becky lost count of the number of bugs that fucked her, touched her, made her cry. The vibration of the viewing crowd—every bug present watching, waiting—only added to the frustration. Every once in a while Wings would come back to check on her, and every time she would smile through her tears and say yes, and would be so thankful for how lucky she was. The last few times, instead of closing her eyes she gazed up at Elshob, into the spider's eyes, and watched herself. She hoped that Elshob liked what she was seeing as much as Becky did.

Finally Wings climbed onto her, lowered itself between her legs, and Becky sobbed again because she thought that relief was near. She was exhausted, so hot and wet—the blankets beneath her had long since soaked through from her juices and the juices of all the bugs—she needed release. Surely Wings would give her what she needed. Wings breached her pussy with its curved backside, dripping with want, and Becky sighed as it pressed inside and towards that spot that always, always made her scream... and then passed it, and rubbed against another spot instead.

Becky did scream then. She screamed with frustration, and with the last of her strength she struggled against Elshob's claws, trying to pull herself away.

Elshob immediately let go and backed away, and Wings pulled out and climbed off her as well. The room was completely silent. All eyes were on Becky.

21

"Please," she pleaded, she begged, "please, just let me come. I don't know how it is for you, but this is a long time for me without an orgasm. It's making me sad. Please." Becky paused, gazing across at the giant spider, and noticing that it's backside was still dripping, leaving a small puddle on the ground underneath where it crouched. Becky looked at her through her eyelashes, hoping she looked as pitiful as she felt. "Please, Mistress Elshob. I promise to be good."

There was a shimmering chitter that flowed through the room, and a moment later Elshob was back on top of Becky, holding her down, only this time the spider lowered herself between Becky's legs, lined up her dripping abdomen with Becky's dripping pussy, and pushed.

The protrusion entered Becky and filled her up, seeming to grow just as big as it needed to be to reach all of her. Becky's pussy was stretched to its limit and it was absolutely perfect. Elshob stilled for a moment, and then pulled out slightly and pushed in again with a thrust that made Becky gasp and her eyes roll back in her head. Elshob did it again, and again, thrusting faster and faster as Becky relaxed and let it happen. She was being used but it was what she wanted, what she needed, and it was almost enough. The little spiders on the wall shivered and trembled, joining their mistress in her pleasure. The sounds of their trembling filled the otherwise silent room.

"Please," Becky murmured, gazing up into Elshob's eyes. "Please, I've been good for you, I promised, please."

Elshob didn't slow down her fucking, but she released a single chit and one of the smaller worms crawled across the floor and placed its little sucker mouth around Becky's clit. The sensation of cold suction from the worm's mouth coupled with the strong and steady thrusting of Elshob's abdomen was exactly what Becky needed. The warmth, which had been building up for what felt like hours, finally bubbled over and Becky came so hard that her vision went white with pleasure. Then everything went black, and she passed out.

When Becky awoke the room was empty, everyone but Wings and Elshob had left. Wings was wiping her down with a warm cloth, and Elshob was gently tucking her under fresh blankets.

"Thank you, Elshob," Becky whispered, snuggling down into the warm softness of her bed. "That was wonderful. Will I see you again? I think my boyfriend would like you."

Elshob chittered, in her deep, strange voice, and although Becky couldn't understand what she said she thought it sounded promising.

Wings and Elshob patted her head one last time before scuttering out of the bedroom and back into their home in the caverns below. Becky slept, and dreamed of spiders.

Chapter Four

When Becky went to the grocery store, Chad was in the kitchen, whistling along to the radio and prepping dinner.

When Becky got home, a brown paper sack tucked under each arm and a six-pack of beer in her hand, the house was silent. Dinner was prepared, warm on the stove, but the burners had been turned off and the pans were covered.

Becky unpacked the groceries, put everything away as quietly as she could, and then set out to investigate. She was very sure she knew what was happening, the only questions were *where*, and *who*.

She went upstairs first—a narrow hallway with a small bathroom directly across from the top of the stairs, and a bedroom on each end of the hallway. There was nobody there, nothing there.

He wasn't on the main floor—the open format connecting the living, dining, and kitchen areas would have made it obvious. So that left only one other place: the basement.

The door to the basement stairs was closed, and as Becky pulled it open—with a slight creak that made her freeze and hold her breath for a moment—she could hear movement and sounds in the dim space below. Shuffling, chittering, and, as she waited with bated breath, the unmistakable melody of her boyfriend's moan of pleasure.

Jackpot.

Becky tiptoed down the stairs as quickly as she dared—not wishing to give herself away—and paused at the bottom. The party was happening on the other side of the room, just a few feet from the giant crack that split the stone wall. That wall was built against the side of the mountain—a mountain that was infamous in the area for enclosing strange and mysterious caverns that were rumored to house creatures of unknown and perhaps malicious forces.

Becky and Chad knew these creatures, and they knew better: They were giant bugs, yes, and they were sentient and intelligent, but they weren't evil. They weren't looking to hurt people, or cause trouble.

They were just horny. They were big bugs, and they liked to fuck.

That was just fine, because Becky and Chad liked to fuck, too.

As Becky's eyes acclimated to the dim light of the basement, she could see more clearly what was happening at the other side of the room. Chad was there, kneeling on the ground, and his head was thrown back in what she recognized as ecstasy. He was surrounded by a crowd of giant bugs—beetles, ants, butterflies, moths; things with wings and things with legs and things with shells and things without. They were large, much larger than normal bugs—two to four feet long, most of them. They surrounded him, not touching him, but they were clearly very interested in what he was doing.

What he was doing was keeping himself very still while a giant millipede sucked his dick.

As Becky lowered herself onto a step, where she could watch the rest of the event in relative secrecy—none of the others had noticed her yet—Chad moaned again, a high-pitched thing that made Becky think he was probably getting close to orgasm.

"*Millie, holy fuck,*" he cried, and Becky pressed her thighs together as the gang of bugs chittered quietly and shuffled in place. They knew it was coming, too.

Becky could tell that Millie was redoubling its efforts, sucking Chad's dick harder, plucking his balls with her mandibles, and it didn't take much longer after that before he came with a shout. Sometimes Millie would let him come inside her, but this time she pulled away, and although Becky couldn't see she could imagine how it looked, Chad's cum pulsing out of him in three or four spurts and making wet patches on the dirty ground.

The bugs went crazy, their chittering reaching a frantic pace as they surged forward to clean up the mess on the ground. Millie and a few others tended to Chad, rubbing up against him and chattering soothingly as he came down off what had looked to Becky like a very satisfying orgasm.

She stood and he looked over and smiled at her, giving her a little wave.

"Hey sweetheart, I made dinner but then I got distracted."

She walked over, careful to avoid the giant bugs milling about on the ground. Some of them greeted her joyfully; they were already heading back into the crack to their cavernous home.

"That's okay. It looked like fun!"

"It was fun!" He stood, tucked himself away, and gave her a kiss. "I'm glad you got to watch."

"I'm glad I got to watch, too."

She hoped next time she'd be able to join in.

Chapter Five

BECKY LOVES FUCKING CHAD when she's on her period.

She loves the scent, warm and organic, and the additional slickness provided by the blood. She loves the mess, how the blood coats her thighs and Chad's groin, his thighs and hips, like he's being marked as hers. They've developed a ritual for dealing with the mess; the laying down of towels beforehand, and the specifics of cleaning up after. But most of all she loves how tender her body is during her period. Her nerve endings seem to be more sensitive, all over her body but especially inside her pussy. Chad's dick feels different inside her during her period than it does during the rest of the month, and when her period starts each month the first thing she wants to do is get his dick deep inside her, and come on it.

Luckily, happily, Chad feels the same way she does. He loves her, and he loves her body and he loves her menstrual blood.

Three weeks after their first experience with their downstairs neighbors, Becky got her period. After dinner, Chad carried her upstairs and went down on her until she cried for him to stop. Then he wiped the red off his face and he started to fuck her. He was taking his time, on his knees between her legs; they were both entranced by the sight of Chad's dick, wet with red, sliding in and out of Becky. They were so entranced that they didn't notice they had a visitor until it started chittering.

It was Wings. Becky loved Wings. She thought it was beautiful, with its shining compound eyes and shimmering green wings and a curved backside that was more often than not dripping with liquid, in anticipation of a fuck. Tonight, Wings wasn't dripping, and there was something about the noise it made that made Becky think it was concerned. It had climbed up on the bed next to them and was pointing its antennae anxiously where their bodies were joined, and coated with blood.

"I think it thinks we're hurt," Becky murmured, and put out her hand to comfort her friend, patting it along its black, shiny head. "It's okay, sweetheart, this is normal. It feels good. See?"

And as Wings watched Becky touched herself, plucked her nipple and rubbed fingers against her clit, while Chad pushed against her thighs and fucked into her harder. It didn't take long for her to reach orgasm, and by then it appeared that Wings was convinced. Liquid was beginning to drip from its backside, and it chittered happily when Becky and Chad came together.

Chad pulled his dick out slowly, and they all watched as it landed, heavy, wet, and coated with red, on the towel laying on the bed under them. He smiled up at Becky.

"Do you want to give Wings a turn? I think it would like to try.'

Becky laughed, because of course she would; she was pretty much always going to play with Wings, given the chance. So Chad backed away and Wings climbed on, wrapping its legs around Becky's torso before lowering its curved backside to the opening of Becky's pussy and pushing inside.

Wings' body was shaped differently from Chad's dick, and she appreciated that difference. It was quite narrow at the end and got very thick very quickly, and that thickness stretched Becky's inside in a way that could be uncomfortable. But her period seemed to have rendered her stretchier, and the blood combined with Chad's cum rendered the movement smooth and glorious. With Wings' front legs on her nipples and its back legs playing with her asshole while it fucked her deep and hard, Becky was in heaven.

It felt so good she didn't want it to stop, but of course it couldn't last forever and far too soon another orgasm was approaching. She came hard, with a shout and a sudden burst of warmth inside her that had her worried that perhaps the bug had goofed and accidentally planted some of its eggs inside her. But no—the warmth was her own, and Wings had dutifully pulled out and deposited the eggs in a pile, between her legs, down on the towel, and it screeched its own pleasure.

Becky petted and kissed the bug as they came down together, and Chad gathered up the eggs and flushed them down the toilet. He returned with a warm, damp cloth, which he used to wipe up the blood and other fluids while Becky and Wings giggled and chittered together.

And then Wings departed, and Becky and Chad went to sleep.

Chapter Six

CHAD LIKES TO DRAW. Nothing fancy, just pencil doodles, sometimes pen—whatever he has handy. Something to keep his hands busy and to help him pass the time.

The evening before this day, Chad and Becky had been visited by some of their downstairs neighbors; Mothra had come, and Eddie. Mothra was a giant moth, who had beautiful silver wings edged in black, and fluffy black antennae that were like giant feathers extending from its fuzzy head. Becky was a fan of Mothra, who was nice to pet and who had an enormous proboscis that it would unroll and use to fuck them both.

Last night it had used it on Becky. It had fucked her with that proboscis and stroked her clit and lips with its antennae, and Chad had watched them while Eddie fucked his ass.

Eddie was one of the many and varied winged things. Wings, with its shimmering green wings and matching eyes, was a special one, but there were many more that were plain black, still shining and beautiful but really all the same. Eddie was special, too; Eddie was red, a bright, shining crimson that Becky once said reminded her of lipstick, or nail polish. Eddie had a curved, tapered backside, and last night Eddie had been horny, dripping and rough. It had climbed on Chad's back impatiently, pulled his hair and scratched his back and screeched, its wings shaking violently, filling the room with a vibration that danced in their ears and made the air spin around them. Eddie had fucked Chad so perfectly that he'd come untouched at the same time that Becky had her third orgasm around Mothra's glorious proboscis.

It had been a wonderful night, and Chad was trying to draw it.

He thought he'd done a pretty good job with Becky and Mothra. He'd captured his girlfriends' curves, her soft breasts with nipples pointing at the ceiling, the expression on her face, eyebrows pulled together and lips pursed. It's a look that could be one of deep contemplation but he knew better; it was the face that she makes just before her eyes snap open and she starts keening in anticipation of an amazing orgasm.

He'd avoided drawing her hand entirely by tucking it into the crook of her knee. He was proud of coming up with that work-around. Drawing hands is *hard*.

Mothra looked good too, its wings pushed behind it and its proboscis unfurled and enough of it outside of Becky's body that the viewer could clearly see just how thick it was, could imagine how it was stretching Becky inside, probing and sucking and rubbing deep inside her pussy.

That proboscis feels good in Chad's ass. He could only imagine how it feels for Becky.

He'd just started drawing himself and Eddie on the lower half of the paper, when a voice came from over his shoulder.

"Jesus, Chad, what the hell is that?"

Chad turned the paper over quickly and turned around in his chair to face his nemesis: Bradford Bates, the ginger terror. Bates was the other lead programmer in their department, and they were at each other constantly. They both wanted the head supervisor post, and they knew their current supervisor, Sam, was applying for new jobs so it was only a matter of time. They were always looking for ways to one-up each other, or put each other down.

"It's nothing," Chad growled, gripping the paper in his fist, cringing internally at the sound of crumpling paper, and thrusting it into his desk drawer.

"It didn't look like nothing," Bates replied, leaning on the divider and raising an eyebrow. "It looked like bug porn. It looked like Becky being fucked by a..."

Chad stood suddenly, crowded up against his nemesis and glared down at him. He wasn't that much taller than Bates but he was much broader and more muscular, and he flexed his arms to make that point.

Bates paused, and Chad leaned forward and breathed into the other man's face.

"By a *what*, Bradford?"

Bates backed away, eyes wide, clearly terrified by Chad's reaction.

"Nothing," he squeaked, "never mind."

Bates skittered away like one of the bugs, turning back to spit a "sick fuck" at Chad when he was far enough away for comfort.

Chad took the drawing back out, tenderly flattened out the creases and looked at it. He admired the lines of Becky's body, the feathery plumes of Mothra's antennae. He remembered the previous night, how much fun it had been, how delicious it was to watch Becky and Mothra as Eddie had pushed him to his limit.

And then, carefully, he thought about Bates, his obvious disgust at the beautiful drawing. Chad had been shocked, surprised and embarrassed, and he thought that maybe Bates would tell other people, their other co-workers and maybe even their boss. It would be humiliating, everyone knowing that Chad draws pictures of his girlfriend fucking giant bugs.

What a fucking weirdo.

Chad was already excited from the drawing, but thinking about his co-workers laughing at him for being a creep excited him more. He stood up and, doing his best not to draw attention to himself or his impressive erection, carried the drawing with him to the single bathroom that was assigned to any gender.

As he pulled his dick out and spat in his palm, he thought about Bates whispering to their supervisor. The embarrassed flush in his face mirrored the purple head of his dick, and he loved and hated how good it felt to squeeze the bulb and run his hand roughly along his shaft. How disappointed everyone at work would be if they knew he was masturbating in the bathroom, thinking about their disappointment. It was a beautiful, horrible cycle, and it went straight to Chad's dick.

It didn't take too long for him to come, tears in his eyes, biting his lip so he didn't make too much noise. That just added to the experience; the gross creep, masturbating in the bathroom as he thought about everyone making fun of him because his girlfriend fucks bugs.

Chad gave himself a moment to breathe before he washed up and put himself away. It had been humiliating, having Bates see his picture like that, but he'd got a good orgasm out of it, and in the end he had the upper hand: it was wonderful to fuck bugs, and he and Becky had nothing to be ashamed of.

Chapter Seven

THE SOFT ONE IS in the food-place.

We call it the food-place because it is the place where they eat food. They, like the others of their kind, are particular about the places they do things. The food-place, the sleep-place, the rest-place, the wash-place.

We are not so particular, but we don't mind if they are.

The sleep-place is frequently the fuck-place, but we have discovered that they are willing to fuck in pretty much any place.

The first time we met them they were in the rest-place, and the second time—when they first allowed us inside their bodies—they were in the sleep-place. But since then, we have had them in every other place in their abode, including on our doorstep.

We have not had them in our abode, and we want them there, which is why we are here now. We are going to take the soft one, soon, we will pick it up and carry it into our place. The hard one is away, but it will be back soon, and when it gets here, we think that it will come looking for its other self.

And then we will have them both.

This was the soft one's idea. It read us a story about another one who was taken away, held captive until its other self came for it. We liked that story very much, and they liked it too, and after we agreed to do it ourselves.

The soft one is preparing a meal in the food-place, and we are gathering outside the door. Not all of us, but enough of us to do what needs to be done. Our mistress and the others are finishing preparations.

There is sound in the food-place—they often have sound, when they prepare meals or rest or fuck—and the soft one is swaying its body to the beat of the sound. We enjoy the sound too, but we avoid moving along to it, lest we draw its attention. Because we have discussed doing this, taking it and keeping it for a while, we believe we have their yes. Yes is very important to them, and so it is important to us as well. We want them and we need them to want us too, and the *yes* is what we need to have them.

It has been such a very long time since anyone else has given us their *yes*, and we do not take it for granted.

We watch it sway, swing its legs and its hips and its arms and shoulders and head. The soft one is making the sound, too, and we think it derives pleasure from it in a way that is similar to how we derive pleasure from its body. We know every part of it, all its soft bits, inside and out, the warm delight of its smooth skin, so unlike our own, every sensitive point we can touch or stroke or prick to make it quiver and moan and cry and scream.

Its liquids are sweet and its pleasure is our greatest joy.

We watch it sway and think about how it feels under us, around us, how it tastes, how it looks at its other self and how they look together, how they smell when they are fucking each other or when they are fucking us, and it is making us excited. Too excited. We need to take it soon, take it through the crack in the wall and into our home where we can show it how we do it when we are in control.

It still does not know we are here.

One of us skitters quickly across the floor, and the soft one looks down at us with a smile and a greeting on its lips that is quickly quieted when we sink our forcipules into its ankle and release a small amount of venom into its skin. It is not enough to damage it, but it is enough to put it to sleep. Before it collapses, falling where we have quickly gathered to keep it from harm, it cries out in pain and surprise. We cherish its cries of pleasure and its pain gives us none; we gather it in our wings and legs and antennae and mandibles and we carry it away with as much care as we can. We will make up for the pain; we will make it feel better soon.

It is warm and soft and sweet even in sleep, and we cannot wait until it can be with us, and awake. And then its other self will come, the hard one, and it will be with us too.

We carry the soft one down the stairs and through the crack in the wall. We are taking the soft one home.

Chapter Eight

WHEN CHAD GOT HOME from work the house was empty. Except for the kitchen, which was full of smoke.

He turned off the burner under the pan and swore, opening the window to let the room air out. He was annoyed at the mess but also excited, his dick already tenting his jeans, because he was pretty sure he knew what this was. Becky's truck was parked out front; she hadn't gone anywhere. And she would never leave a pan on the hot stove on purpose. The only other alternative was that the bugs had taken her.

It was her own fault. A week or so before, she'd been reading a book of Greek myths before bed. She had just started on Orpheus and Eurydice when a few of their friends had come up from the basement to see if they wanted to play. Becky hadn't been in the mood to play but she had been in the mood to read, so she had read and editorialized and given the bugs her own interpretation of the myth, which ended quite differently than that traditional story.

After all the storytelling it turned out she'd been in the mood after all, and Chad and the bugs had worked together to give her a few orgasms, as a kind of thank you. But the bugs were clearly taken with the concept of a woman stolen away to the underground, to be saved by her true love, and once he and Becky understood what they wanted they gave them their most hearty consent.

Chad's dick was painfully erect by the time he reached the crack in the basement wall. It had been narrow when they'd first moved in, an annoyance more than anything, and they'd originally planned to fill it with concrete. After they'd met Millie and Wings and the others that plan had changed, and the crack was now wide enough for Chad to climb through. Loose stones and mortar and unopened bags of concrete laid scattered around the dusty floor.

Back on his feet on the other side of the wall, Chad clutched himself through his jeans and listened. It was not silent in the cavern beyond, but instead of the sounds of the monstrous bugs—shuffling, chittering, screeching—the only sound Chad could hear was a low and very human moan. As Chad listened the moan grew louder, into a cry, through which he could just make out a flurry of words: *yes* and *fuck* and *Wings* and *oh my God oh my God oh my God*. The crying ended with a shout—not of pleasure, but of frustration. *Goddammit!* Becky yelled, followed by a loud chorus of chittering that sounded an awful lot like scolding to Chad's ears.

She was quiet for a moment, and then she sniffled. He could imagine her tears, her frustrated pout that couldn't hide the fire in her eyes, and he finally unzipped his jeans and pulled out his dick. He palmed it as Becky promised to be good, over and over again, and a soft shuffling suggested a rearrangement of bodies deeper in the cave.

"Who's that?" Becky's question floated through the gloom. "Ant? Mothra?" Her guessing was interrupted by another moan, which steadily grew to another babbling cry. This time they allowed her an orgasm, her scream of release accompanied by a chorus of joyful chittering and the unmistakable smack of multiple clutches of eggs splashing against the stone floor.

Chad came too, cum spilling on his hand and dripping onto the ground. He imagined Becky bound in spider's webs, only her pussy and ass, mouth and breasts exposed, covered with giant crawling bugs of every species. They would poke and prod her, penetrate her, taking and giving pleasure and there would be nothing she could do but scream.

A soft noise near Chad's feet drew his attention. A single worm was there in the dirt—one of the worms with a mouth like a vacuum, which it put to excellent use on Becky's clit or wherever else it was needed. It was sucking Chad's cum off the ground, but when it was done it looked up at him. The worms didn't have eyes as far as Chad could tell, but the way its head tilted somehow indicated curiosity.

Chad shook his head.

"Not yet, little one. I think you would all like more time to play Hades to our Eurydice before Orpheus tries to claim her back."

He crouched, lowering his hand so the worm could suck the rest of the cum off it. He trusted the bugs to take very good care of Becky, for as long as they wanted.

"I'll be back in a minute with some food and fresh water that you can take to her, but I'll be sleeping in our bed tonight, if you need me later."

The worm wiggled at him and disappeared into the darkness.

Chad went upstairs to make a sandwich.

Chapter Nine

BECKY WAS PRETTY SURE she'd only been with the bugs for a few hours, but it already felt like forever.

She was bound with webs, which Elshob had been gently wrapping around her when she'd first awakened. While she was passed out, they'd undressed her and coated her body and hair with some kind of oily substance, which she guessed was designed to keep the webbing from sticking too closely to her skin; the webbing was very, very sticky, and reminded her of narrow strips of double-sided duct tape, but stretchy. When the process was finished, she felt a bit like a mummy, except that her legs were wrapped separately so they could be spread wide, as they were now. Her arms were bound to her body, hands overlapping on her stomach. Her breasts were left bare, as was her ass and the area between her legs. Her head was wrapped as well, all but her mouth and nose covered by the sticky stuff, which smelled of dust.

They rearranged her regularly, repositioning her body and her legs so she never cramped or had to hold a difficult position for too long. They had made her drink water and had fed her dinner not long after she awakened, and more food some hours later—human food, not anything buggy, for which she was thankful—so she knew that Chad was bringing it to them. He was playing along, and she had to admit that the thought of him in the house, alone, thinking about her down here with their friends, was very exciting indeed. Had he listened at the crack? Had he laid awake in bed that night, stroking his dick and thinking about Becky being fucked by Wings and Eddie and Millie, the ants and beetles and moths and everyone else who took their turn with her body?

She hoped he had. She hoped he would come to watch. Maybe he had; maybe he was just very quiet. Maybe sometimes when the bugs were chittering and shuffling around they were doing it to hide his footsteps.

Becky had been thinking about these things for a while, but another thought was beginning to push Chad out of her head, a more immediate concern that was potentially very embarrassing.

She had to pee.

She'd had to pee when she was making dinner. She'd thought about it, had decided that it wasn't too bad and that she'd wait until the risotto was done and she didn't have to constantly stir the rice. But then the bugs had come for her, bitten her ankle and carried her away and wrapped her up and given her orgasms, and she'd stopped thinking about it. But now it was many hours later and she'd had many sips of water and the urge was strong.

The urge was very strong.

Becky was hanging, facing the floor, her hips slightly higher than her head, which seemed to help the situation a bit. They'd left her alone for a while—a few hours, maybe, it was so hard to tell—and she'd taken a nap. Or, she thought she had. With the webbing around her face, covering her eyes, and floating in the air... she expected the sensation was a bit like being in a sensory deprivation tank.

Once she'd noticed she had to pee it was hard to ignore. That single fact took up all her attention. She was thinking about it when she heard the familiar shuffling of the bugs returning to her, as she recognized the movement of her own body in space as the webs holding her in place were cut, and as a collection of legs and bodies—familiar, but not recognizable—lowered her to the floor, turned her over, and then raised her up again to be hung once more.

She had to pee.

In her new situation Becky's legs were once more spread wide, her head now higher than her hips, a cross between sitting up and lying down; it felt like lying on the chair at the dentist's office, before they tipped it back to start the teeth cleaning. It also shifted her organs around, applying more pressure on her bladder than there had been before.

She had to pee so bad. She tried to wiggle, to reposition herself in a way that might relieve the pressure, but she was bound too tightly and it wouldn't have mattered anyway. Her bladder was full and there was only one way it was getting empty. Tears of pain and humiliation welled up and were lost in the webbing that covered Becky's eyes.

It was time to fuck again, apparently, because someone—she was pretty sure it was Eddie, because it kept thrashing its wings, and it wasn't as careful with the sharp ends of its feet as Wings and most of the other winged bugs usually were—climbed up on her tummy and proceeded to rub its curved end between her legs. It was dripping, and the creature carefully dripped and then used its body to spread the fluid on her, between her legs. Her own body responded despite the discomfort, and she moaned and did her best to lift her hips and rub against Eddie too. In a few minutes, satisfied with her moisture, Eddie would press its tip into her, deeper and deeper, stretching her, filling her. It would feel amazing and she wanted it, but.

She still had to pee.

Becky tried to shift her attention away from her full bladder, which felt ready to burst. When Eddie breached her, shoved its end into her opening and tenderly pressed deeper, and deeper, she almost forgot that she had to pee. But as it worked her, using one foot on her clit and others attending to her breasts—she couldn't ignore it any more. In order to come, she was going to have to relax. But if she relaxed, she would pee. It was a conundrum that left her edging for long enough that the gathered insectoid crowd began to vibrate and chitter softly. She almost thought she could understand them. They were curious, concerned; afraid that something was wrong. Why was she holding off for so long?

And Eddie—it seemed to take her hesitance as resistance, and it only worked harder. It scraped more keenly against her g-spot, rubbed around her clit in exactly the way they knew she loved the most. She could have said no, could have told it to stop, but she didn't want to stop. She wanted to come as much as they wanted her to.

Eventually it was just too much. Becky screamed, and let go. Two releases hit her at once, overwhelming the lower half of her body with warmth. The pressure of the piss through her urethra, so close to her vagina, seemed to increase the strength of her orgasm, which went on and on, much longer than even the best usual one.

She was dimly aware that the reaction the bugs had to the sudden discharge was nothing less than hysteria. Even as she was still pushing the piss, the creatures were in a frenzy. Eddie (she was positive now that it was Eddie), caught by surprise, let out a shrill squeal but very quickly

43

had to pull out, and Becky clearly heard its chitty grunt and the wet smack as its eggs hit the floor below. That one had clearly appreciated the fountain, but the squeaking and shuffling and excited chittering of the bugs on the floor told Becky that they had enjoyed the shower, too.

Becky laid her head back and finally encouraged all her muscles to relax. Another drop of urine escaped and joined the tracks running down her butt, and she sighed contentedly.

Chapter Ten

THE BUGS HAD TAKEN Becky into the basement on Friday evening, and it was now Sunday morning. Chad had been keeping himself busy. He'd attempted to take care of some things around the house he'd been meaning to tackle—the running toilet in the guest bathroom, the squeaky stair, the window in the upstairs hallway that wouldn't quite close—but he found himself drawn into the basement. He'd spent hours standing in the dim, dusty space, next to the complete darkness of the crack, listening to Becky crying her pleasure while the horde chittered and cheered and spilled their eggs on the stone floor of the cavern.

Chad found himself thinking about those eggs a lot. He'd become very familiar with them over the past months, watching them drop out of their friends, the shape and size and amount varying, depending on the species of the things. The beetles had relatively smaller, slightly yellow oval-shaped eggs, while the eggs of the ants were round and more of a grayish-white. Elshob's eggs were large and round and dry, and those of the winged creatures were the same approximate shape and size but were always accompanied by a large amount of liquid.

Chad liked all the eggs, but he was particularly fond of the eggs of the winged ones. It was the liquid; slightly , and very slippery, it was a wonderful lubricant and the effect of the deposit was enough like human ejaculation that he sympathized with it. Watching Wings or Eddie or one of the other ones drop a clutch of eggs after making Becky cry with pleasure was almost as good as having an orgasm himself.

The very first time they'd fucked the bugs they'd immediately agreed to a single rule, and that rule was NO EGGS. Neither Becky nor Chad had been interested in being incubators for buggy babies, and they still weren't, but after seeing how the creatures treated their eggs—as a mess to be cleaned up, occasionally as a snack—they were less concerned than they had been at first about the issue of receiving the eggs. They'd even talked about doing it—giving Wings permission to drop eggs into one of them, just once, just to see what it was like.

Yes, Chad had been thinking about those eggs a lot.

Chad was finally ready to go behind the wall, , to play Orpheus to Becky's Eurydice. To bring her home. He hadn't even changed out of his pajamas, just in case he had a reason to undress (he had no idea what the bugs had planned for him; they knew he would be coming down although they didn't know exactly when). He'd cooked breakfast, a cheese and bacon omelet, and his dick had hardened as he cracked the chicken eggs and new, highly stimulating thoughts about the eggs of the horde began to swirl in his mind as he mixed them with milk and spices and beat them with a fork until they were frothy. He'd eaten his breakfast and then made another omelet to bring down to Becky, along with a hot mug of coffee. He'd been bringing her water and sandwiches all weekend, and he was sure she'd be ready for a nice hot meal.

Chad was still thinking about the eggs as he approached the crack in the basement wall, plate and mug and cutlery in hand. There were noises through the crack, the shuffling and chittering of the giant bugs, and the softer tones of Becky's voice. She was speaking although her voice was so quiet Chad couldn't understand what she was saying.

Millie came out of the crack as Chad reached it. It was almost as though Millie had been waiting for him, expecting him, and he thought that was a little weird but he was also very glad to see it because to be honest he was a bit uncertain about going through the wall by himself. It was just very dark, on the other side of the wall, and he said something to this effect to Millie. Millie froze, and seconds later a soft glow alighted at the other side of the wall . That was weird, but welcome, and when the monstrous millepede turned around and headed into the tunnel, towards Becky's voice, Chad straightened his shoulders and followed.

They didn't go very far, just through the rough-hewn tunnel—barely tall enough for Chad, he had to duck a few times to avoid hitting his head on the ceiling, and maybe twenty feet long—and into the first room of the cavern. It was higher than the tunnel, perhaps twice as high, and much wider, although stalactites and stalagmites projected from the floor and ceiling here and there, like giant tusks growing from the earth. The space continued further into the mountain, there were several openings visible on the back wall, darkness emanating out of them, but the bugs had taken advantage of this space to host their guest.

The first thing Chad saw was Becky, suspended face-down in the center of the cave, three feet or so from the ground. She was completely wrapped in spider's webs. Well, almost completely wrapped. As Chad's eyes got used to the dim glow—a soft greenish-blue coming from groups of what he assumed were glow worms in the corners of the room—he could see her naked ass, almost directly in front of where he stood. Her legs were spread wide, and there was her naked pussy, too. The room was so dim it was difficult to tell its color, but it looked dark to Chad, dark and swollen, and it glistened deliciously in the glow.

"Chad?" Becky called, lifting up her head. He took a step sideways so he could see her better. She was bound tightly; even her head was covered, apart from her mouth and nose. Her breasts were bare as well, and a little worm hung from each of them, although they didn't appear to be doing much work.

"Chad, are you there or am I hallucinating? I swear I smell coffee." She sounded tired but lucid. Her voice echoed eerily around the cavern.

"I'm here," he answered, taking another step closer. For the first time he noticed the gathered horde, a carpet of every kind of bug, covering the floor as far as he could see. They moved aside to make room for his feet. Elshob was perched on a high shelf up on the right side of the cave; she was surrounded by her entourage of normal-sized spiders, which wriggled like a wave against the stone wall. He nodded at her, and she waved a foot at him.

"I brought you breakfast, and I want to take you home."

"Ah, Orpheus has finally come to claim his Eurydice. You're lovely, Chad, but you need to wait. Wings and I were just getting ready to fuck again. Would you like to watch?"

It was a silly question, and they both knew it. The bugs knew it too, and they chittered good naturedly as they led him to a boulder where he would have a good view of the show. There was a flat part next to where he sat, and he placed the plate and mug there. Millie settled on the other side of him, pressing against his hip like a dog.

Wings flew in from the dark depths of the cavern. Chad had never seen it fly before, and it made an impressive noise, like a helicopter, as it swung around the ceiling and finally came to rest on Becky's lower back.

Wings's curved backend was dripping, large drops fell to the ground like the start of a rainstorm as it flew around, and that made Chad think about the eggs again. He imagined Wings depositing the eggs inside Becky instead of releasing them on the floor. Would she enjoy it? Would it make her come? Could she even hold them all? Would he be able to fuck her, if her pussy was full of eggs?

This is what Chad was thinking about as Wings pressed its backend into Becky's pussy and started to thrust. He could see the worms on her nipples, and he could tell the moment they started to suck because they started to wiggle, and immediately Becky arched her back and cried out. She didn't stop crying, and her shouts—in time to the rhythm of Wings's thrusts—echoed around the space and mingled with the chittering of the horde, which was becoming louder by the moment.

This continued for several minutes. Becky was holding out, and it was beautiful to see. She'd always loved delaying her orgasms, and his, too, and the bugs had become the best sandbox for finding new methods for denying herself. She was very close, every creature in that cave could tell, and she let out what Chad assumed would be her final cry of orgasm.

It wasn't. Instead, she shouted, "Wings! Give me your eggs!"

Pandemonium.

The bugs cheered like they were at a Big Ten football game and their team had just scored a touchdown. For its part, Wings did as it was told, and instead of pulling out it deposited its clutch of eggs inside Becky's pussy with a screech. The process took several seconds, since Becky's body offered resistance that a release into the air didn't. Chad sat, breathless, and watched as Wings thrust into Becky's body several more times, pushing the eggs in with each thrust. Becky whined, but held still and took it.

When Wings was done the two of them, woman and bug, rested together for a moment, and finally Wings pulled the tip of its backend out of her. A single wet egg slipped out and plopped onto the floor below. One of the beetles scurried out, grabbed it, and scurried back, cradling it like an ancient relic.

Wings crawled up Becky's body to her head, and as it checked on her well-being, Chad got up to check out her ass.

"Are you okay, sweetheart?" He asked, as he reached out and stroked a finger against her swollen lips, stretched around an egg that barely peeked out of her opening. It was white but glowed green in the light of the glow worms. He was reminded of a toy he had when he was a kid, a stuffed thing with a friendly smile and a head that glowed when you squeezed its body. It was a strange thing to remember given the circumstances, and Chad tried hard to forget.

"I'm fine," she replied, her voice slightly strained. "It feels good? I think? Weird but good."

Chad pressed against the egg and it gave slightly but didn't move, and Becky groaned.

"Please don't do that, Chad, there's no room."

"That's a shame. I was hoping I could fuck you with the eggs in." He really was disappointed. His dick was so hard—it had stiffened up when he was cooking breakfast, and had only gotten harder during the intervening minutes. He could fuck her now, no problem. Given the way the bugs were still gathered around them, the center of their attention, Chad thought they wanted him to do it, too. "Maybe you can push a few out, so I can fit my dick in you?"

She shook her head vigorously and groaned again.

"I want them in me for a while. I feel so full, it's nice. And they're Wings's eggs, you know? I like having them there. You can still fuck me, though." She wiggled her backside, as well as she could given how she was trussed up, and it took Chad a moment to understand her meaning. But once he did, he was more than happy to go along with her.

Filled with eggs Becky's pussy was leaking copious amounts of slick fluid, and Chad took advantage of it, scooping it onto his fingers and rubbing them against the furled muscle of her asshole before slipping in one finger, and then another. She was suspended at exactly the right height, his hips lined up exactly with hers, and Chad wondered if this was purposeful on the part of the bugs. Another silly question; of course it was. Given how tightly the eggs filled Becky's pussy her ass was surprisingly relaxed, and very soon Chad, holding her hips steady, was able to slip the head of his dick inside her.

51

They'd played around with double penetration before, with toys and although Becky had been DP'd by the bugs, Chad hadn't been involved with that. At least, not yet. Fucking Becky's ass with her pussy full of eggs felt similar to that, only moreso. This was much tighter than it was even with the largest dildo they owned, and Chad was trying so hard to be careful, and gentle, to not push too hard, when Becky growled out in frustration. "Just go in, Chad, I can take it!"

He trusted her, so he did.

He pressed all the way in, until his hips bounced against her cheeks and rested there, fully hilted. She whined, and wiggled her backside against him. He held her tighter; the skin where his fingers dug into her turned white, and glowed in the eerie light.

The worms, still attached to her nipples, started their work again—Chad could tell, because as before she arched her back, and her internal muscles tightened up too. It was on the edge of too tight, but he held her steady and whispered to her, and began to move inside her. Not thrusting, but a gentle back and forth, just barely, just enough to encourage her to relax. Movement caught the corner of Chad's eye; another worm had made its way up one of the stalagmites that Becky's shoulders were suspended from, and was crawling along the webbing. When it reached her it crawled down her back, and then around her waist and down. Chad lost sight of it, but he was pretty sure he knew where it was headed. He continued his gentle almost-thrusting while Becky moaned and cried and did her best to wiggle in her wraps. The bugs watched on silently, but the air was charged with the energy of expectation.

Not even a minute later Becky seized up again, muscles tightening; the worm had found her clit, and was apparently giving her exactly what she needed, because she let go with a scream. Her inner muscles clenched around Chad, and at the same time the orgasm pushed the eggs out of her body, and they landed on the floor with that familiar wet *plop*.

The bugs went crazy again, and the room filled with their chitters and squeaks and the vibrations of their wings and bodies. The sound, the sensation of the eggs moving through Becky's body, the sound of them landing on the ground, the way her muscles gripped Chad's dick as she came—all of these things combined to push him over the edge, too, and he came into her with a shout of his own.

The horde loved that, too.

Chad helped them take Becky down. They'd managed to keep her relatively clean, although she was covered with some kind of oil, and she was full of smiles even though her legs were very unsteady. The omelet was cold, and so was the coffee, but that was okay; Chad would make her more.

They said goodbye and thank you to their friends, and headed back up into their house.

Chapter Eleven

CHAD HAD A TWIN brother named Brock. Brock was coming to visit the couple for the first time since they moved into the new house, and Becky was nervous.

Becky was always a little nervous leading up to Brock's visits, but then she would feel silly after he left, because his visits always turned out to be fun. They were always very fun, even though it was guaranteed there would be at least one knock-down, drag-out fight between either her and Brock or Brock and Chad during the visit. But the fights always ended with sex—animalistic, passionate, occasionally violent sex—and they always made up after.

That was one of the things that made his visits so much fun.

This time, Becky was mostly nervous about the bugs. They were a part of her and Chad's life together, and they couldn't bear to hide them away; it would be a lie. Becky was also worried about offending them; she didn't want them to think that she and Chad were ashamed of them, because they weren't. Not at all. Becky adored the horde, and so did Chad, and they both hoped that Brock would like them too.

Brock arrived late on a Friday afternoon, driving up the gravel drive and parking his black Mustang between Becky's old pickup and Chad's Subaru Outback. He was dressed all in black, including his old leather jacket that still carried the slight aroma of cigarettes despite the fact that he'd quit smoking two years before. The dark waves of his hair stroked his shoulders and the dimples in his cheeks creased as he gave Becky a smile that made her cheeks feel warm and her pussy relax. Chad saw it happen, and grinned behind his hand before giving his brother a hug and a kiss on the mouth that would have shocked their mother.

"How was the drive?" Becky asked as Brock followed her into the kitchen, Chad taking his bags up to the spare room on the second floor.

"It was fine," he replied, settling himself on a stool at the island while Becky went to the stove to stir the chili. "The traffic was pretty bad right around Richmond, but it always is." She hummed and stirred, only half listening to him. She was thinking about the bugs. She had told Wings and Eddie that Brock was coming, but she was never sure how much they actually understood.

Hot breath against the back of her neck and warm hands around her waist brought her attention back to the present.

"What is it, baby? What has you so distracted?"

"Nothing."

"Nothing?" He sounded skeptical. "Sure doesn't seem like nothing from where I'm standing." His hips pressed against her backside; his erection was long and hard against the crack of her ass through his jeans and her thin yoga pants.

Becky leaned forward and pressed back against him. She couldn't control the moan that escaped her throat as she thought about how good Brock's dick would feel inside her. It was pretty much the same size and shape as Chad's, but he wielded it differently than Chad did his. Chad's dick was an extension of his person, a representation of his love for Becky. Whether he was using it on her or on Brock or with the bugs, it was all for her, because he was hers and his pleasure was hers, too. Brock's dick, on the other hand, was a tool, or a weapon. He used it to get off, and to get other people off.

Becky adored Chad, but she loved to fuck his brother.

Chad came into the kitchen then, and he was hungry and Becky was hungry, so they decided that they would eat first and then play for dessert. Becky tried to catch Chad's eye but he seemed to be avoiding her. They still hadn't decided how exactly they were going to breach the topic of the bugs with Brock.

After dinner, they relocated to the living room where it became clear that Chad's approach was to get Brock very drunk and tell him when his defenses were down. Unfortunately, it didn't work out exactly as planned, because getting Brock drunk just made him horny, and giggly, and after a while all three of them were wearing nothing but their underwear, and were lying on the living room floor kissing and groping each other in various rotating pairs. Between gropes and sips of rum and Coke, Brock was telling them about his new boyfriend.

"He's just so fucking sweet," he insisted for the fifth or sixth time, voice slurred as he rubbed his brother's dick through the thin cotton fabric of his boxers. "He's cooked for me a couple times, and he listens to me—really listens, you know? And I listen to him too." He paused groggily, and pulled the elastic of Chad's boxers down just enough to expose the round head of his dick. "Fuck, guys, I'm so fucking horny. Talking about George is making me fucking horny. Are we going to fuck, or what?"

Becky had only been half-listening again, her mouth on Chad's neck and a hand in her panties while she watched Brock fondle her boyfriend. Chad was sipping a gin and tonic—his third, or maybe fourth, it was hard to keep track—and his cheeks were very red. The head of his dick was purple. She was thinking about how easy it would be for her to slip off her panties and slip onto that dick when a noise from the hallway captured the attention of all of them.

Becky and Chad froze. Brock frowned.

"That is the biggest fucking millepede I have ever seen in my life," he said slowly. "Four feet long? Five? Is it real? Or am I so fucking drunk I'm hallucinating?"

Chad cleared his throat. "Um, yes. It's real, a real giant millipede."

Becky answered as cooly as she could. "We call it Millie. It lives in the basement."

Brock was still frowning, but he didn't seem freaked out, which Becky took as a good sign.

Millie, on the other hand, was clearly excited. It chittered and undulated into the room, its little legs scuffing softly against the hardwood floor as it approached them. Millie aimed for Chad, and Brock scooted back as the giant arthropod climbed over his brother's legs and rubbed against the head of his dick—still hard and purple, poking out of his boxers—before looking up at him and then over at Brock. It chittered again, looking back and forth between them.

"I think Millie's confused, because you look alike," Becky guessed. "Maybe it's never seen identical twins before."

Chad reached out and took Brock's hand, and Brock, drunk and a bit overwhelmed, allowed him to lower it to Millie's head.

"Woah," Brock murmured, as Millie felt his fingers with her mandibles and then pulled them into its mouth. "Woah."

"Yeah," Chad replied. "Do you want it to suck your dick?"

Brock's eyes bugged out of their sockets. "Did you say it would suck my dick? I am too fucking drunk, dude. Maybe I should just go up to bed."

"Oh Brock, come on," Becky urged, getting up on her knees and crawling around to the other side of him. "Millie sucks Chad's dick all the time, and he really loves it. And I love to watch it." She said the last bit in the most sultry voice she could muster, right in his ear, with her hand nudging below the elastic of his boxer briefs so her fingers could just barely stroke the very tip of his dick. It was erect, and leaking precum; her fingers came away wet and sticky, and she rubbed them over his head, slicking it all up.

"I've never fucked a bug before," he admitted, lifting up his hips to allow Chad and Becky to tug down his underwear.

"We fuck them all the time," Chad said, his voice full of pride. "We have a regular menagerie under the house; ants and beetles and spiders and things with wings and worms and even butterflies." He stroked his hand up and down Brock's shaft while Becky kissed Brock's neck and twisted his nipples tenderly. Millie was getting impatient, and it released a chittery squeal and bounced on Chad's lap. He gripped Brock's dick at the base of the shaft and lifted it up; Millie lunged forward and took the dick into its mouth with a squeak.

"Oh fuck," Brock moaned, his hips raising up automatically. "That feels good. Fuck."

"Yeah, Millie's really good at sucking dick," Chad confirmed.

"I still don't believe this is happening," Brock murmured, closing his eyes and leaning into Becky. "I'm just fucking drunk. Too fucking drunk." But he wasn't too drunk to have an orgasm, which he did a few minutes later, shouting as his dick shot cum into Millie's mouth and it drank the fluid down with a gleeful squeal.

Very soon Millie was gone, back into the cavern where Becky supposed it would tell the other bugs all about the new human in the house, who looked so much like the other one and who was also down to fuck. Brock was half passed-out, leaning back against the sofa and softly murmuring about fucking bugs and how drunk he was.

Chad and Becky traded a glance; Brock had had enough for one evening. They helped him stand up and they all clamored upstairs, leaving the glasses and bottles on the living room floor. They could clean up tomorrow, and hopefully after his baptism by Millie, Brock would be willing to meet the other bugs, too.

Chapter Twelve

ALL THREE OF THEM knew there would be a fight eventually. The only questions were: where, when, and what it would be about.

The answer to the first question was: in the kitchen, quickly moving to the living room; to the second question: on Sunday afternoon; and to the third... Well, Brock wasn't exactly sure. Becky and Chad had been arguing in the kitchen, and then he walked in, and Becky said something and then Chad said something and then he said something back and the next thing he knew Becky was pummeling his chest with her fists and yelling and he backed into the living room and was trying to hold her—but not too hard, because he didn't want to hurt her—and he said something to Chad and Chad yelled at him and he yelled back and Becky growled and then he tripped over a chair and landed on his back and Becky fell on him and... well, long story short he ended up with his jeans down his thighs and Becky was completely naked and riding his dick like he was some kind of breeding stock and Chad was standing by holding a bag of ice on the side of his face.

It was good. This was one of the reasons Brock visited his brother, and they all knew it. Brock and Chad had started fucking when they were teenagers—they were close, best friends, and sex felt good, it wasn't that deep— and it wasn't until Becky that either of them had a partner they felt comfortable letting in on their arrangement. It had happened through a strange series of coincidences, and Brock thought about it as Becky bounced on his dick, swearing and angling herself so he was hitting her exactly where she needed him, and he tried not to come.

Brock had met Becky first—most people didn't know that, but it was true. She'd been a waitress at the place where he'd tended bar, from college until he finally figured out what he wanted to do with himself that wasn't fucking around and being a dick. She'd been young—barely 21—and he'd been ten years older and an asshole. She was bad at her job, and he gave her shit, and she gave him shit back, and when they closed together he'd pull her into the single-stall bathroom and set her on the sink, and she'd call him names and pull his hair and tell him how much she hated him and he'd go down on her until she couldn't breathe.

She'd quit after a few months, and Brock... She'd featured in his masturbatory fantasies for ages after, but he certainly never thought he'd see her again. About a year later he got a call from Chad, telling him about this amazing girl he'd met—love at first sight, blah blah blah—and isn't it funny that she knows you? And of course it was Becky. She'd walked up to Chad on the street all prepared to pick a fight, and he'd been adorably clueless and instead of fighting they'd gone for coffee, and then dinner, and then they got an apartment together.

Awwwww, so adorable.

Chad had brought Becky home for Christmas four months later. Brock and Becky had ended up having a screaming fight on Christmas Eve while their parents had been at church, and that fight had ended

61

in a threesome in the basement—to Becky's surprise and delight. That visit had pretty much set the tone for their relationship moving forward. Every few months for the past five years Brock would visit, they'd laugh and mess around, then they'd break shit and fuck like animals, and everything would be fine.

Brock dated a lot, but he hadn't been in a relationship with anyone he was comfortable sharing with Becky and Chad. His new guy... he thought, maybe. His name was George and they'd been dating for a few months. They'd met at the gym, of all places. George asked him for a spot, then he asked for a coffee, and then he'd asked him home. George was sweet, and hot, and very open minded. Kinky. He'd said some things in passing when he found out that Brock had an identical twin brother that led Brock to believe he at least wouldn't be disgusted by the incest, and he knew that George was bi, too, so if he thought Becky was cute and she liked him too they might be willing to... the vision of his boyfriend fucking his brother's girlfriend floated across Brock's mind, and the concept was so appealing he had to bite his lip to distract his attention from the pressure still building inside his dick.

Brock was so deep inside his own head that it took him a minute to notice that someone else had joined them. Well, something—he opened his eyes to see that Chad was crouching, and perched on the floor next to him was a green and black thing, shining, with shimmering emerald wings and compound eyes that looked at him with undeniable intensity.

"Fuck," he said. "What's that?"

Becky had seen it, too, and just like that she was up and off him, leaving his dick to flop back onto his stomach with a pitiful wet smack. Brock swore at his rapidly cooling dick as he watched Becky crawl over to the thing and give it a hello pat. It skittered closer to her, and Brock could finally see its backend, which was long and thick and curved under its body. It was dripping fluid, which made a real mess on the hardwood. Becky and Chad didn't seem to care.

"This is Wings," Becky said, turning back to Brock and lowering her front, while lifting up her hips. "Wings is going to fuck me now, if you want to watch."

Since the thing with the millipede on Friday night—Brock hadn't seen any more bugs, although he thought he'd heard them skittering around once or twice. Brock had been sure was a dream, until Becky and Chad reassured him at brunch the next day that, indeed, they had a horde of giant sentient bugs who lived under their house and who fucked them regularly.

On Saturday night when he and Chad had fucked around after Becky had gone to sleep, he was almost positive he'd seen eyes shining at them out of the darkness, and heard muted chittering when Chad had finally had his orgasm in the back of his throat.

"Yeah, okay," Brock said, the tone of his voice purposefully not quite carrying the extent of his excitement, and he sat up and started to pull up his jeans until the expression on his brother's face told him not to. So instead he pulled his jeans down and off, and Chad set aside the bag of ice he'd been holding against his face and took his jeans off, too. By this time the creature had climbed onto Becky's back and was using the softly pointed tip of its backend to tease her pussy, which was already swollen and drenched from her ride on Brock's dick. It rotated its head around so it could stare at Brock. Chad stared at Becky and the bug, squeezing the head of his dick in his fist. Becky moaned in anticipation.

The thing—Wings, they'd called it—pushed its backend into Becky, who squeaked, and Brock could only stare as her pussy stretched to conform to its girth. After a pause—during which Becky was making some pretty incredible noises—it started to thrust. Her moans grew louder and changed to match the pace of the fucking, which made its own sound, a wet squelch accompanied by dripping of fluid from between Becky's legs onto the wooden floor below. Before long quite a puddle had grown there. Brock was amazed.

Chad's voice in his ear made him jump. "Wings can make her come without touching her clit. I can't do that. Have you ever done that to her?"

Brock, who relied almost entirely on clitoral stimulation to make women orgasm, shook his head mutely, and continued staring down at Becky getting fucked by a bug. His brain was telling him that it shouldn't be arousing, that it should instead be gross and disgusting, but Becky's body was telling him something else and his body agreed entirely. It had been quite a while since he'd been so hard, so ready to fuck.

He wanted to fuck a bug. No—he wanted a bug to fuck him. He wanted a bug to fuck him exactly like that bug was fucking Becky. She was crying; Brock couldn't see her face, but he could hear her sobs, and imagine how the tears looked, streaming down her pink, swollen face. If Brock knew her orgasmic tells—and he did, he really did—she'd be coming soon. And when she did, it would be one he wouldn't forget for a while.

Chad's hand on his dick distracted him. He squeezed his head, then moved down to tug on his shaft. Brock looked into his brother's face; he felt almost drunk.

"Do you want to be fucked like that?" Chad asked him, his breath warm against his cheek. Brock nodded, and glanced down at Chad's mouth. He'd smacked that mouth, earlier, during the fight, but now he just wanted to kiss it. So he did, he pressed his mouth against his brother's and bit his bottom lip before sucking his tongue into his mouth. Chad moaned, and squeezed his dick again, pressing it up against his own.

"I bet Wings'll fuck you, if we ask it nicely," Chad murmured into Brock's mouth, "once it's done with Becky. Would you like that?"

"Yeah," Brock answered, looking back at Becky. "I would like that very much."

"Good. Because I want to see it."

They didn't talk more, because Becky was gearing up to have an orgasm. She was lying almost completely flat on the ground, her legs spread very wide, knees up beside her hips, which were tilted towards the ceiling. Wings, perched on her highest point, was thrusting faster than any human Brock had ever seen, and it was loud—squealing, squelching, its wings vibrating so fast their hum permeated the entire room. There was a scent, too; the smell of Becky during sex, which was familiar, but something else too. Organic, and dark, like dirt and something more.

Very suddenly Becky threw her head back and screamed, a babbling scream of pleasure full of half-spoken words, fuck and Wings and Chad and even, he was sure, Brock, which made Brock feel unreasonably proud of himself. He didn't have long to feel proud because as soon as Wings had finished working Becky through her incredibly intense orgasm it pulled out of her and, with a mighty squeal, the tip of its backend opened up and a large number of very wet, round objects dropped out of it and landed on the floor with a smack .

Brock jumped back and fell onto the sofa.

"What the fuck! What the fuck is that!" He'd learned about insects in school, but he still hadn't expected *that* .

Chad, who was now kneeling on the floor attending to his girl-friend, tried very hard to suppress his laughter.

"It's just eggs, man. Just eggs. Wings'll clean them up itself. See?"

And as Brock watched, even more amazed than before, Wings turned around, hopped off of Becky, and proceeded to chow down on the eggs like it was popcorn at the movie theater. Or something. Like very wet and slimy, very large and round popcorn.

It was disgusting, but no more disgusting than actually fucking a bug, so Brock decided he wasn't going to be too judgmental. When it was done, Wings skittered over to where Chad was holding Becky. Brock thought it looked like it was checking on her, making sure she was okay, and he thought that was pretty cool. His dick was still hard as a rock, and he stroked it as he watched the aftercare. It was sweet—very sweet, Becky and Chad together were always so fucking sweet, it was enough to make his teeth hurt—but he had a need and he hadn't forgotten what Chad had said earlier.

"Hey Chad," Brock called over to them. "Do you think that thing will fuck me now?"

Becky, who had missed their entire conversation, gaped at them.

"What?" She cried. "You're going to let Wings fuck you? That's wonderful!"

Chad looked down at Wings.

"Hey, Wings, do you want to fuck my brother?" He pointed at Brock, and the creature followed his gesture, setting its intense gaze on Brock yet again, and on the impressive erection jutting out of his lap. It was clearly not some dumb bug—this thing was intelligent. It was wise . The realization made Brock shiver, but he still wanted it to fuck him in the ass.

Wings tilted its head, chittered briefly, and then skittered quickly into the hallway and down the stairs to the basement.

Chad shrugged.

"I guess that's a no. Sorry, man."

Brock shrugged too and tried to be cool, although he was surprised at how much he was hurt by the rejection.

"That's okay. Can I fuck you instead?"

"Yeah, sure," Chad replied nonchalantly, although judging by the state of his dick, he wanted to be fucked as badly as Brock wanted to fuck him. Becky did a happy dance, and reached into the drawer of the end table for a bottle of lube that they always kept handy, just in case.

Chapter Thirteen

BECKY WAS RELAXING ON the sofa with a pint of Chunky Monkey and watching Brock ease the head of his dick into his twin brother's slicked up asshole when there was a clatter on the stairs and yet another giant bug skittered into the living room. This one looked very similar to the one that had fucked Becky—Wings—only instead of being green it was a lustrous scarlet, with the same shining compound eyes and gleaming wings and enormous, curved backside that dripped fluid all over the hardwood floor.

"Hey, Eddie," Becky said around a mouthful of ice cream. "Are you here to fuck Brock in the ass?"

The thing chittered, and regarded Brock with the same intensity that its... brother? Whatever, Brock didn't know how the bugs were related to each other, and he didn't really care. Anyway, it was intense and wise and Brock wanted the slick, pointy end of its body in his ass. He wasn't sure he could even imagine how it would feel, and having his dick pressed tight in his brother's ass while that thing reamed his own ass in turn... he couldn't really imagine a better way to spend a Sunday afternoon.

Actually, yes he could. If he could do that with Becky's pussy on his tongue, that would be better. But she was eating ice cream on the sofa, and he was standing behind where Chad was bent over and resting on his arms on the dining table, so it didn't look like eating Becky's pussy was going to be part of the equation. Another time—there would always be another time.

Brock held Chad's hip with his left hand and pushed his ass cheek aside with his right hand, and pressed in another inch or so, enjoying the way his brother moaned quietly, muscle clenching around his dick.

"So good," Chad murmured, his knuckles white where his hands were in fists on the table top. "Your dick always feels so fucking good."

Brock rewarded the praise with a short thrust that made Chad's breath hitch, and then gave him another inch. He always eased it in slowly, an inch at a time, pausing several times to rest. One, because he loved Chad and he didn't want to accidentally hurt him, and two, because it got Chad so hot and frustrated that sometimes he'd beg or even cry before Brock got his whole dick inside him. Brock liked it when Chad begged and cried, so he'd go as slow as he could bear to see if he could make his brother do it.

Brock hadn't forgotten the giant bug, though, and it hadn't forgotten him either. It climbed up onto the table first, and chittered softly while it got close to Chad and peered into his face.

"Hey, Eddie," Chad said, words transforming into a moan as Brock slid another inch of his dick through the tight ring of his asshole. The red creature redirected its attention to where the men's bodies were slowly joining, and reached out with one of its antennae to gently poke, first against Chad's stretched rim, and then at the base of Brock's cock. Brock barely felt it. Then, before he realized what was happening, the thing the others called Eddie climbed up and over him, and gripped him on either side of his back with what felt like little claws. It almost hurt, but in a good way.

Brock leaned over his brother's back, pushing him flat on the table, and pushed the rest of the way into his body. His hips rested comfortably against Chad's soft buttocks, and he rested his cheek between Chad's shoulder Brocks with a sigh.

The thing chittered and squeezed its claws as it began to probe Brock's asshole with the tip of its backend. It was slick, but also cold. Brock was a bit surprised at how cold it was, the thick, slimy substance that the thing was using to prepare him for its girth.

"Hey, man," Brock whispered to his brother. "My plan is to just relax and let the bug do its thing. It'll move me, I move in you. Okay?"

"Yeah, that sounds good," Chad replied, his voice muffled where his cheek rested against the tabletop. "Hope you enjoy it—Eddie can get a little bit carried away."

Brock wasn't worried—he was confident he could handle whatever that giant red bug might have in store for him.

It started easy. Eddie was being careful—the same kind of careful that Brock was with Chad. The kind of careful that could be tender care, but could also be a simple attempt to heighten arousal. Brock didn't really care which one this was; it felt fucking amazing. The thing didn't feel like a dick, or like any dildo he'd ever used. It was hard, and slick, but it had a certain amount of give. It was quite narrow at the point but got thick very quickly, and Brock appreciated Eddie's slow penetration when it finally got to the point where his body simply couldn't accept any more of the bug.

The thing paused, and let out an unworldly squeal, high-pitched and eerie. Becky, still feeding herself mouthfuls of ice cream on the sofa, widened her eyes and tucked her knees under, sitting up on her haunches and assuring herself a good view of the proceedings.

"Oh, wow, Eddie must really like how you feel, Brock, I haven't heard it make that noise before. This is gonna be fun." She turned the spoon over and sucked it onto her tongue.

Eddie started to thrust. Unlike Wings, who fucked Becky with shallow, quick thrusts, this one seemed to favor longer, slower thrusts. It pulled its backend almost all the way out of Brock's ass, and then shoved it back in so quickly that it knocked Brock's breath out of his lungs, and Chad's breath in turn.

"Fuck!" Chad exclaimed. "That was good."

"Yeah it was," Brock agreed, as Eddie pulled out again, maybe a little more quickly this time, and then thrust in again with a squeal. It seemed to Brock that the bug understood that it was, in a way, fucking for two, and it intended to take that responsibility seriously. It continued to thrust, speeding up slightly with each one, and very soon it had reached a pace that was almost enough. Almost, but not quite; it had both men shaking and begging for more.

Glancing in Becky's direction, Brock saw that Becky had abandoned her ice cream—the almost empty container lay dripping and forgotten, next to her on the sofa. The spoon was still in her mouth, but she didn't seem aware of it until her boyfriend let out a particularly loud and guttural cry and she bit down on it. It bounced against her teeth, hard, and she threw it across the room and jumped to her feet. She was clearly enjoying it, but it looked like it wasn't enough for her either. She wanted to be part of the show, and she knew exactly what she wanted.

She stepped around the coffee table as quickly as she could, and climbed up onto the dining table in front of Chad. Chad kept his eyes closed, his cheek resting sweetly against the wooden table, mouth open and releasing a soft cry with every thrust the giant bug transferred through the body of his brother.

Brock watched as Becky, still naked from her earlier escapades, spread her legs and tapped Chad on the head. When he lifted it up so he could look at her, he came face to face... Well, her pussy was in his face.

"Hey, baby," she sighed, spreading her pussy lips apart and pushing the hood down to uncover her clit. "Will you eat me? I want to come, too."

Brock's mouth watered as his brother lifted his head just enough so that Becky could scoot under his face, and he sighed in sympathy when Chad put his mouth on her pink slickness and began to feast. He could smell her, sweet and salty with a little bit of tang, and he could hear the noise of his brother's lips and tongue against her skin, his humming sounds—interspersed still with his cries when the thrusts reached him. Becky was beautiful, laid out on the table like a dream, her hair a fucking mess, Chad's hands up holding her knees wide, one of her hands between her legs holding her lips open for him, her other hand toying with first one nipple, then the other.

Brock stared at her; he couldn't help it. She was smiling, and moaning, and looking right at him.

It was quite a thing for Brock, to be fucked by a bug while fucking his brother and watching him fuck his girlfriend with his mouth. It felt amazing, everything about the experience was amazing. Eddie, with the huge, thick, slick bug ass? Eddie was amazing too. Eddie knew how to fuck.

Every thrust now was somehow rubbing right against Brock's prostate, and with that plus the visual—and the aural—of Chad eating Becky out, he was going to come very soon.

"Hey Chad," he murmured, "you getting close?"

"Yeah, close," he answered breathily, "but my hands are full, I'm gonna need a reach around."

"I got you, bro." Brock sat up just enough to worm his hand around his brother's body, and gripped his cock in his fist. Eddie saw what was happening, and everything happened very quickly after that. Chad came first, Brock was pretty sure, hot cum spurting out of his dick and across Brock's hand just a few seconds after he grabbed it. Brock was next; he could feel his ass clenching around Eddie's backend, and he came hard inside his brother's ass. When he pulled out his dick was followed by a sweet stream of cum. There was a lot of it; Brock was proud of his cum.

Once Brock was done, Eddie let out another one of its intense squeals and pulled all the way out, a move followed by the unmistakable sound of a clutch of eggs smacking wetly on the hardwood floor. It didn't freak Brock out the way it had the last time; in fact, he felt a little proud. He was pretty sure that bugs didn't really have orgasms, but the egg dropping was a sign of joy, or something, and he was pleased to have been at least somewhat responsible for that. Eddie hopped down and had a snack of its own.

Becky came last, wriggling and crying on the table. By the time she reached her orgasm her fingers were tangled in Brock's hair and his tongue was in her mouth and Eddie's mandibles were pinching her

73

nipple and Chad's tongue was all the way in her pussy and it was clear that whatever else happened she was going to sleep very well that night indeed.

Once her cries quieted and the men—and bug—were finished congratulating themselves on a job well-done, Eddie slipped back downstairs and Chad carried Becky up to bed so she could take a nap. Brock slurped down the dredges of the ice cream and threw out the container. He was glad that they'd moved to this new house, and they had the fun new friends in the basement. He had to leave the next day, but he was already looking forward to his next visit. If things continued to work out with George, he thought, as he gazed out the window at the orange sun shining low against the grass of the front lawn, he might bring him along next time.

Chapter Fourteen

BECKY WALKED INTO THE kitchen just as Chad was setting the glass top down on the old Crock-Pot he'd been gifted by his mom when he'd gone off to college. He was speaking softly to Wings, who was perched on the back of a chair that was pulled up next to him, in front of the kitchen counter.

"Once you make sure the pork shoulder is fully covered by the soy sauce mixture, you turn the Crock-Pot on here," he turned the dial to *on*, "and then set the timer here." He pushed the timer so it read *6:00* and the machine beeped. Wings hopped on its perch at the sound, and Becky giggled. They both turned to look at her, Chad's expression growing into a mischievous grin.

"What are you guys doing?" She asked, leaning against the door jamb.

"Wings came in while I was preparing dinner, so I thought I'd show it how we do things upstairs."

Becky laughed, and then she caught a whiff of what was in the pot. "Is that what I think it is?" She nodded at the pot and took a few steps forward. Chad tossed the measuring cups and bowls he'd used to prepare the sauce into the sink and turned on the water.

"The Asian barbecue with extra garlic? You bet. I know you love it, and I like to give you what you love."

Becky gave Wings a pat, and it chittered and rubbed its front limbs together. She watched Chad wash the dishes and set them in the drainboard, then use a towel to wipe down the countertop.

"Tah dah!" He yelled with a grin, hanging the towel on the oven door. "All clean.

Becky hummed. Watching Chad, and the fact that Wings was present, had given her an idea.

"What are you guys doing now?" She tried to be nonchalant, but the look that Chad gave her and the way Wings vibrated under her fingertips made it clear that they were all in the same book, if not exactly on the same page.

"Well," Chad answered slowly, taking a step towards her, "since you're here, and I'm here, and Wings is here, I thought we might have some fun."

Becky held back a smile, but she couldn't hold back the warmth and pressure between her legs.

"Oh yeah? What kind of *fun* were you thinking, baby?"

Chad glanced at Wings, then back at her, and then he took her elbow and led her into the living room and towards the stairs up to the second floor. Wings chittered, dropped to the floor, and skittered after them, its wings quivering in anticipation.

"Well, I was just thinking about that time, back in our old apartment, when we spent all afternoon in bed. Do you remember that?"

Becky *did* remember that. They had, in fact, spent many afternoons together in bed, but he was talking about one specific afternoon. The week before they'd been messing around, and Becky had squirted. She'd never done it before, and Chad had never been with someone who had, and they'd been both fascinated by it; but were completely unsure about how it had happened. So Becky had done a bit of research and had come up with an article that had explicit details on *how to make your woman squirt,* and they'd decided to try it.

It worked. Boy oh boy, *had it worked.* They'd soaked the sheets and towels and each other, and Becky had had more strong orgasms in a row than she'd had before or since—even including the time the bugs had taken her into the cavern. It had also taken a lot of Becky's energy, and Chad had ended up having to ice his hand that evening, so it wasn't something they'd done again to that extent. But it sounded like Chad wanted to do that again, and Becky didn't have anything else going on, so okay.

"What is Wings doing?" Becky asked as they walked together up the stairs and she started the process of removing her clothing.

"Wings is going to watch," Chad answered, pausing at the linen closet in the hallway to pull out a stack of towels. "I'm going to show Wings how I do it, and then we can see if it can do it, too. Okay?"

Becky agreed that this was a fantastic idea, and she took a minute to pee and give herself a little wash before laying down with her butt on the towels that Chad had laid out, and they got to work.

Well, Chad got to work. Becky laid back and did her best to relax.

He started by going down on her, which was always nice. A couple of orgasms against the soft warmth of Chad's mouth had Becky melting, and that's when he put his fingers inside her pussy and started stroking her G-spot. Wings perched on the footboard, head cocked, shining compound eyes gazing where his fingers disappeared into her pussy.

That's all it took, really—long and continuous pressure against her G-spot. But the trick was *long* and *continuous,* which was work for Chad, and although it felt good it always felt weird for Becky to have that pressure, in that place, for so long. She had to remind herself to relax, which was, ironically, a little bit stressful. But Chad was perfect, as always, whispering sweet words and calling her *beautiful,* giving her an occasional kiss on her clit or a suck on her nipple. Wings watched intently and , interjecting every once in a while with a flutter of its wings. And always, always, that constant pressure on her G-spot.

Becky had her first orgasm after five minutes or so. Maybe more—it was hard to tell. The orgasms she had from this stimulation were always intense and loud, and when Wings squealed along with her it filled her with joy.

Once she was through the first orgasm her initial instinct was always to tell Chad to stop, to have him pull his fingers out of her. But she knew that wasn't what her body needed—her body needed him to keep going, if they had any chance of a gusher. So she bit her lip, and Chad kept up that steady movement, and after just a few minutes the pressure had grown to overflowing and she was crying out again in pleasure.

This orgasm lasted longer—or maybe it was lots of little ones strung together, it was kind of hard for Becky to tell. Either way it hardly mattered. Wings squealed through it, and Chad continued his steady working inside her, and she rode it out until finally it wound down and she could relax again.

Only she couldn't relax, because Chad was *still* working her.

Becky had lost all track of time, and she was feeling a bit loopy. She wasn't really sure if she could even have another orgasm—that second one had drained her pretty well—and she said as much to Chad. At least, she opened her mouth to say as much, but the words that came out were maybe not even words at all. He seemed to understand her, in any case, because he said, "No, baby, we're gonna keep going until you squirt Wings in the eyes," and it took less energy for her to just agree and let him keep going than it was to try to make him stop. Besides, she wasn't sure she really wanted him to stop. It still felt good, very good, and as he kept up that steady stroking against her G-spot the warmth and pressure started building again, and Becky thought she might have one more orgasm in her after all.

This one took a little longer to build up, but it was worth it. As the warm pressure grew inside Becky, she gripped the sheets in her fists, and wiggled her hips to press herself more closely against Chad's hand. He tutted, and draped his left arm across her body in an attempt to hold her still, but it had the additional effect of pressing down on her pelvic bone, which meant even more pressure on her insides. This made her cry—at this point she was sobbing, gripping the sheets and sobbing like a baby. Chad was sweet, telling her over and over what a good girl she was and promising to stop after the next one, whatever happened, pressing his lips against her temple and her cheek, and Wings was concerned too. It hopped down and skittered over next to her, patting her gently with its limbs.

"I'm good, Wings," she managed to murmur through her dullness. "This is really, really good."

The end came quite quickly, the warmth and pressure hit a sudden peak and then Chad was urging her to, "bear down, baby, bear down!" She did, and a wave of pleasure overwhelmed her as a wave of warm wetness streamed out from between her legs, dousing her, a visibly pleased Chad, and a very surprised Wings. The giant bug clearly hadn't understood exactly what was going to happen. It let out an extended screech, shook its wings—scattering liquid all over everything—and dropped a clutch of eggs right onto the bed.

Once she'd worked through her orgasm Becky laughed. She felt good—really good—and not nearly as exhausted as she thought she would. Chad got to work cleaning up the eggs—Wings had been so overwhelmed that it didn't even notice the eggs, it just stood there, quivering and rubbing its front limbs together.

"You okay, Wings?" Becky asked it, reaching out a finger to touch the claw of its front limbs. It looked at her and chittered happily. Wings had learned something new, and Becky hoped that it would take that new knowledge back with it to the horde. Maybe things would be more interesting in the future; Becky hoped so.

Chapter Fifteen

THIS IS ONE WE have not seen before.

We know the soft one, and the hard one, and the hard one that is a clone. There have been others, but they are long gone.

This one is new. We watch it from our hiding places. It is in a big machine, and we are already considering what we can do about that machine when it walks around the abode and looks in one of the covered holes.

We do not like it, this one. It is sneaky. We think it is not here for pleasure.

It is what we call an intruder.

When we have an intruder, we have things we do to protect ourselves. The soft one and the hard one are not us, but they are ours, and we will protect them as we would protect ourselves. We need them, we need to protect them.

It will be a gift. A gift for them.

Becky usually worked from home, but today she had a special meeting to attend in town. So instead of waking up at her leisure and slipping behind her computer with a cup of coffee at 9am, she was up and dressed and out the door alongside Chad at 7:30am. They kissed each other goodbye, she climbed into her old pickup, he got into his Subaru Outback, and they both drove into town.

Becky was home at 4pm, and was greeted by the warm scent of her favorite meal—Crock-Pot Asian barbecue pork shoulder. She smiled to herself as she set down her bag and shrugged off her coat, hanging it in the front-hall closet. Chad must have sneaked home earlier and set it up as a surprise. Becky was definitely surprised, but it was a good one.

She was less pleased when she got into the kitchen and discovered that he'd left it in just a bit of a mess. The measuring cups and bowls had been tossed into the sink but he hadn't cleaned them, and there were ragged streaks of sauce across the counter and even a few on the floor. Well, maybe he'd been in a hurry—he only had an hour for lunch, and they were a good twenty minutes outside of town, so he would have had to do it in a rush. And it was a very sweet thing to do. So Becky tidied up with a smile on her lips, and went ahead and set the table so she wouldn't have to worry about it later.

Chad arrived home two hours later, just as the timer on the Crock-Pot was going off.

"Hey, that smells amazing!" He shouted in from the front hall.

"It sure does!" Becky shouted back, pulling a platter of roasted vegetables out of the oven and placing it on the table before returning to the stove to dish the rice into the bowl that Chad had brought back with him from his trip to Japan the previous year. The bowl was blue

82

and gold and was decorated with white bunnies; he'd picked it up in a shop in Kyoto that he swore only sold pottery with bunnies on them. It was her favorite serving dish, and she only brought it out on special occasions.

Chad walked into the kitchen and gawked at the table. "Wow, this looks great! Thank you!"

Becky giggled. "Thank *you* . It was so sweet of you!" He gave her a weird look and shrugged, then pulled two bottles of beer out of the fridge and handed one to her before sitting across from her at the table.

"Bon appetit!" He started dishing the rice and vegetables while Becky focused on the meat. She'd taken it out of the Crock-Pot and placed it on a platter, and was in the process of using two large forks to pull the strands of grayish-pink flesh apart. She hadn't really noticed before—it was hard to see the hunk of meat when it was in the pot and covered with sauce—but as she worked through it she thought it was a little strange. It was a bit longer than the usual pork shoulder, and not nearly as fatty, and it wasn't until she'd pulled through about a quarter of it that she realized that it wasn't a single hunk of meat after all—it was two smaller pieces pushed together.

"Chad, what cut of meat was this?" She asked, dishing a couple of hearty forkfuls onto the plate in front of her, already filled with rice and veggies, and handing it to him. He traded her with the plate in front of him and shrugged.

"How would I know?"

Becky frowned. That was a strange answer, considering he'd been the one to prepare the meat, but maybe he'd been distracted. And the food smelled amazing, and looked amazing—despite the lack of fat it was still quite juicy—and she dug in, too.

83

Both of them ate what was on their plates, and had second helpings of the meat.

"You know," Becky said, chewing through what was going to be her last bite of the seasoned flesh, "I think this might be the best rendition of this barbecue you've made yet. Did you do something different with the sauce? More garlic or something? It seems, I don't know, extra tangy."

Chad stared at her across the table as though she had two heads.

"What are you talking about? *I* didn't make this, you did."

Becky frowned, and looked at the remnants of the meal on the plate in front of her. A single lonely strand of meat, coated in sauce, rested on the edge of the plate, next to a piece of broccoli.

"I came home and this had been cooking for a couple of hours. I assumed you came home at lunch and did this as a surprise."

Becky's heart sank and an unfamiliar, cold feeling of horror crept up her spine, but before she could think of another thing to say or do, a clatter of hard limbs coming up from the basement announced the arrival of their downstairs neighbors; their friends. They came up the stairs and filed into the kitchen, coming to a stop next to the table.

They were not alone. Well—that wasn't exactly right. They didn't just bring themselves. Amongst them, being carried on the hard backs of a group of huge, black beetles, was a human head. And not just any human head. This head had a face with skin as pale as milk, a pink slash of a mouth, and it was topped by a shock of orange hair.

It was the head of Chad's coworker, Bradford Bates, and Becky was absolutely certain that his body had been the source of their dinner. She was dimly aware of Chad saying, "oh, yuck," as she hopped up from the table, scooted around the gang of bugs that covered most of the floor, and vomited the contents of her stomach right into the kitchen sink. Luckily the sink was empty, and as she flushed it down the garbage disposal she could hear Chad in the bathroom down the hall, doing the same thing.

Once she'd finished rinsing out her mouth, Becky laughed. She couldn't help it; the situation was so horrifying and absurd, but it was suddenly obvious what had happened, and she didn't know what else to do at that moment. She leaned on the kitchen counter and laughed until her stomach hurt, until tears ran down her face and she couldn't breathe.

Chad returned to the door and just stood there, staring at the head of his least favorite co-worker, resting on the backs of the bugs that he liked to fuck.

The bugs, likewise, seemed to be at a loss. Whatever reaction they had expected, this clearly wasn't it. They stood there, too, chittering nervously and shifting from limb to limb, causing Bates's head to roll around slightly on their slick, black backs.

"The bugs killed Bates," Chad finally said, just as Becky was beginning to calm down. "I fucking hate Bates."

His declaration—deadpan, honest—sent Becky back into paroxysms of giggles.

"He must have come to the house," she was finally able to say, wiping the tears from her face with her pretty yellow cloth napkin, still clutched in her fist, "and the bugs saw him as some kind of interloper or something."

"He *was* a fucking interloper," Chad said, shifting his weight from his right to his left foot. "What the fuck was he doing, coming to the house." Chad was angry, his voice growing louder with each declaration. "He saw a picture I drew, of you, and Mothra, and he decided that I was a sick fuck and I guess he thought he'd come to the house and find something disgusting to show Mr. Barnes, to assure that he'd be promoted when Sam leaves."

"Guess he found something," Becky said, with another giggle, and Chad finally smiled at that, although he was still aggravated.

"Yeah, I guess." Chad crouched and addressed the bugs. "Okay, first. That fucker would have hurt you. Forget about my job; he'd have sold you to science labs or something. So it's forgivable that you did this today."

The horde, whether understanding just the tone of his voice or the words themselves, chittered happily, enjoying his praise.

"But," Becky added, crouching down herself, "we don't kill our interlopers. You should *never* kill people. If people you don't know come to the house, you stay away. Understand? Because they can hurt you. And we don't want that." The thought of the bugs being hurt trying to protect her and Chad broke her heart a little, and she made the saddest face she could. The bugs seemed to get it, and one of them reached a limb up and patted her on the cheek.

"We also don't eat them," Chad added. "I know cannibalism isn't a big deal for you guys, but it's a real taboo for people." He stood again and mimed revulsion at the chunk of barbecued Bates still hanging out on the serving platter, holding his nose and shaking his head and putting his hands up as though holding the chunk of meat at bay.

"No eating. Got it?"

The bugs chittered in agreement, and headed back down into the basement. Chad followed them, and he was gone for a while as Becky cleaned up the kitchen and threw out the rest of the barbecued Bates,

86

although she was slightly disgusted to find herself sucking on the serving spoon; the flavor was really good. She wondered if the bugs might have put some additional secret ingredients into the sauce, and then decided she was probably better off not knowing.

When Chad returned he was alone and Becky was naked, left leg splayed over the back of the sofa, teasing herself with a vibrator just enough to leak a bit. Chad got naked quickly, and as he fucked her slowly he told her that the rest of Bates was safely disposed of, and his car as well. There was, he had learned, a very wide, very deep hole in the caverns, accessible through a hidden opening deeper in the woods but not far behind their house. The hole was so deep that even the bugs didn't know how far down it went, and they'd pushed and tossed everything down there. Bates had called in sick to work that morning—Chad had been cc'd on the email—and he lived alone, so the likelihood that anyone had known of his whereabouts today was very low.

This news made Becky happy. She loved Chad, and she was very fond of those bugs, and she didn't want them getting hurt. She had never really liked Bates very much, although as her orgasm approached and its warmth finally washed over her, and Chad's breath came hot and fast on her neck, she considered that she had liked him very much, just there at the end.

Chapter Sixteen

CHAD AWOKE TO THE sound of a metallic click and a cold constriction around his balls and dick, accompanied by a giggle.

Not his giggle—it was Becky's giggle.

The bedroom was dim but from the moonlight filtering in through the thin curtains Chad could just see Becky, sitting back on her haunches in front of him. There were a few smaller shapes gathered next to her. She giggled again, and the bugs echoed her laughter with soft chittering. The constriction around his privates continued, and as he sleepily considered his girlfriend, and their playmates, and what this midnight visit might mean, the constriction grew.

"What's up, sweetheart?" He asked, sitting up, and flinching as something cold and hard pressed against his inner thigh.

"Not you," she replied, with yet another giggle. The bugs chittered along with her. "The Window of Opportunity will assure that."

She gestured between his legs, and he finally looked down.

Again, the light was dim, but he could clearly make out the metal device that was fastened around his dick. His balls were in there, too, and when he reached down and gave it a gentle tug he found that it was very securely fastened around him. It was made of stainless steel, and it was very short—just a couple of inches. It was shorter than his dick was when it was soft, and he was a bit amazed that all of him could fit in it, even when he didn't have a hard on. Most of it was solid although there was an opening at the end, and Becky had thoughtfully ensured that the tip of his dick was there. He was not going to use having to pee as an excuse for getting out of this.

To tell the truth, Chad wasn't sure how he felt about it.

Becky obviously didn't care how he felt about it. She leaned down and gave him a sweet kiss on the soft skin that poked through the opening at the end of the cage, and then she started to get comfortable with the bugs on the other side of the bed. She lay on her back, and held her pussy open for the probing of the backend of an ant. Chad noticed a small silver key hanging from a ring threaded over Becky's pinky. He wouldn't be sneaking the key then, either. Damn.

Two beetles attended to her breasts, coupling mandibles on her nipples with limbs on her soft mounds, and a handful of worms had crawled up on her belly and appeared to be conversing amongst themselves to decide which one of them would have the honor of sucking her clit. He turned his attention to them. His dick began to stir its interest, and Chad decided he didn't like it much at all.

He would never get an erection with that thing holding his dick.

Becky was having a good time. The ant was fucking her, or she was fucking herself on it, she was moaning and the ant and beetles were chittering right along in sympathy. The worms had decided which one drew the short straw, because two of the worms had fastened themselves to Becky's nipples—to her obvious delight—and the third was making itself comfortable in the thatch of brown hair between her legs. It was clearly in no rush.

"Oh, Chad," she moaned, reaching out to stroke the cold cage around his dick. The key tapped against the steel as she petted it, making a slight *tink* with each movement of her hand. "This feels *so good*. I love getting fucked, love having something thick and long and strong in my pussy, love getting my cum all over it." As she spoke she thrust herself harder against the ant, and Chad could clearly see that the thing was wet, glossy and shining from Becky's juices and its own, which dripped out of the tip of its backend and spread all over both of them.

The cage was getting tighter, and Chad's cheeks were hot. He was so torn about that cage. On one hand, it was hot. On the other hand, it was *really* uncomfortable. He swallowed, and shifted so he could lie down beside Becky. He kissed her temple, and she gazed at him with her eyes shining in the darkness.

"I love fucking you, you're so hot," he whispered. "Your pussy is so warm, tight, soft and sweet and wet and... fuck, it's perfect. You're perfect, sweetheart. So gorgeous when you come. I love watching your face when you come. I love how you taste when you come. " She preened at his praise. The cage was full by that time, and the ring around the base of his dick and balls tugged uncomfortably as his dick tried valiantly to get hard. Chad willed it to stop, even as his fingers traced across Becky's torso and toyed with her belly button. She spread her knees farther apart.

"You're so sweet, baby," she whispered breathily, closing her eyes as the beetles and worms visibly increased the intensity of their work. "So good to me."

Chad wiggled uncomfortably. "Good to you. Like wearing a cock cage when you know I don't really like to, just to make you happy?"

She grinned, interrupted by a soft cry when the worm between her legs latched its little mouth around the tiny hard knob of her clit.

"I love knowing that you want to fuck me but you can't. You can't even get an erection, can you? Your beautiful dick, curled up and caged, wanting me but not able to have me." Her voice was getting more husky and more breathy by the moment. "You want to fuck me, don't you Chad? If you could you'd pull me off this ant and fuck me on your dick, wouldn't you?"

Chad bit his lip and tried to fight the steady pulsing of the blood between his legs. The cage was really tight, too tight, and if he wasn't careful, soon it would start to hurt.

"I'd do anything for you, Becky. Of course I want to fuck you. Fuck you hard, make you come, hold you down while you come on my dick..."

And at that Becky cried out and writhed one last time, pressing her body against his. The bugs all squealed, the beetle on Becky's left side slightly louder than the others as it found itself sandwiched tightly between the two humans. But it didn't seem to mind too much.

Once Becky had worked herself through her orgasm the ant pulled out of her, but it didn't drop eggs. Instead it turned around and climbed up on her, observing her with interest. The worms, which had likewise removed themselves from her body, wiggled together as though waiting for future instruction.

"How are you feeling, sweetheart?" Chad asked, kissing Becky's lips and enjoying the feeling of her smile against her mouth.

"Feeling good," she answered, amusement bubbling in her voice. "Ready to go again. I could come two or three more times, I think."

"Oh yeah?" Chad lowered his hand to the cage, still hard as ever but now warm from his body heat, and grasped it loosely in his fist. "Ready for me?"

She laughed, a joyful sound, and dangled the key in his face. His spirit raised briefly, until she shook her head and lowered her hand.

"No, baby, not yet. I want you to wait. Okay? Can you wait?"

Chad knew that if he said *no* she'd take the cage off him. She might not fuck him immediately but he could stroke himself, masturbate while she fucked a beetle or the ant again—or both of them at once, which appeared to be their plan. He could come with her, shoot his cum on her chest and then he and the bugs could eat it off her while her breathing steadied and she prepared for another go.

But that's not what she wanted. She wanted him in the cage, held tight, so he couldn't fully enjoy himself. She wanted to control him, and even though he didn't like it, that's what he wanted too. So Chad laid back down and gave her another kiss, and watched as the bugs slowly, delicately, worked the woman he loved to another wave of pleasure.

Chapter
Seventeen

By the time Becky had three orgasms with the bugs it was time to get Chad out of his chastity device. She knew that he'd need a rest after 20 minutes or so of his enormous dick being crammed into that tiny cage—much longer than that could be dangerous—and she had an idea for how she could help ease his discomfort and his annoyance. He hated being caged up, she knew he only did it because she loved it, and she wanted to show him exactly how much she appreciated his discomfort.

Wings and Millie had shown up after they'd gotten started along with a few more beetles, and Wings had demanded the last turn with Becky. Millie, meanwhile, was distressed to see Chad's dick caged up. It curled up next to Chad, pressed up against him and touched the cage delicately with her antennae.

"Okay, baby," she murmured, once he'd helped the bugs wipe up the last of the fluid from the eggs that Wings had deposited across her back.

All Chad could do was moan. Poor thing—his balls were quite swollen and purple, and the end of his dick where it peeped out the end of the cage was swollen and purple, too. Becky lifted up her hand, the little silver key still hanging off her pinkie from a metal ring. She delighted in how Chad's face lit up as he gazed at the key.

"You've been such a good boy. Are you ready to get out? Are you ready for me to take care of you?"

Chad nodded vigorously, his hair flying around his shoulders, and she laughed.

"Okay, hmm... Stand over here," she said, gesturing to the end of the bed, a few steps distant from the footboard. She turned on the bedside lamp as he moved to where she indicated. He stood, his left hand cradling his caged dick and his right hand running through his hair, a nervous gesture Becky adored.

"Now lean over," she commanded, "rest your arms on the footboard."

He was curious, but did as she instructed. She crawled onto the floor under where he stood. The bugs gathered on either side of her so they could see what was going on. Chad leaned over, head down and eyes closed, legs apart so as to avoid crushing his privates any more than the cage already did. Gently, carefully, Becky unlocked the device. She removed the cup first, and then quickly reached higher and unclipped the cock ring, removing that as well. Chad groaned loudly as his dick leapt out and promptly expanded to its usual healthy girth. She was impressed that he'd been able to keep all of that in the tiny cage, and judging by their chittering the bugs were impressed as well. Wings thrummed his wings and trilled especially loudly. Becky expected that it had an idea of what was about to happen, and it approved. Millie hopped forward, aiming straight for Chad's erect dick, but Becky nudged it back.

"Not today, Millie," she admonished the monstrous millipede. "Mine."

Chad started to straighten up, but Becky tutted and grabbed his elbow, pulling him back down.

"No, baby, stay like that. I have a treat for you."

He looked at her from between his elbows. His hair hung down onto the mattress, and he looked funny with his face upside-down. Becky smiled, thinking about the time early in their relationship when they'd spent an evening taking turns lying on the sofa with their heads upside down, eyes drawn on their chins, making stupid videos and laughing until Becky peed her pants. Chad was remembering the same thing, and he made a funny face that made her giggle.

But she had something else in mind.

Still facing Chad, Becky scooted back until she was under where his dick hung down, and then she took it in her mouth, just the head. It was hot, and so large it forced her jaw open. From this angle, looking up to where his dick joined his body, Becky was struck by just how long and thick it was. And she was going to put that entire thing down her throat. *I am*, she thought to herself. *I am hungry for his dick, and I can do it*. Usually when she went down on Chad, Becky used her hands to help touch all of him, but that wasn't what she wanted to do tonight. She wanted to take him *all*.

Although tired from several strong orgasms her body responded to her thought, heat growing yet again between her legs, nipples hardening. The bugs shivered in sympathy.

She held the head of his dick in her mouth for just a moment and then lifted herself up, taking more and more of him until his balls rested on her chin and the tip of his dick nestled in the back of her throat. She stopped, and waited, focusing on breathing slowly through her nose. He was quiet for a moment, and then he said, "woah." Another moment later he said, "fuck," and that was when she snaked her tongue up between her teeth and the base of his cock, and used the tip of it to teasingly lift up first his left testicle, and then his right.

"Fuck!" He said, more loudly, and then, "fuck, *Becky*."

She did that a few more times, licking and stroking his sweet balls, and then she pulled her tongue back in. Saliva had been gathering in her mouth, and she needed to swallow it. She'd done something similar in her practice, but the end of Chad's cock was thicker than the tip of Wing's backend, and she wasn't sure how well swallowing was going to work.

She figured she might as well try, though, so she did. She reached up and grabbed Chad by the hips to steady him, pulled his dick even further into her throat, and she swallowed.

Becky chugged the spit down her gullet, and Chad roared like a bear. The warmth between her legs spiked again, and she was filled with deep satisfaction. She thought he was going to come; he was certainly leaking precum, she could taste the salty bitterness all the way at the back of her throat, but he didn't. He just stood still—bless him—and cried his rumbling cries into his arms, crossed over the footboard. The bugs cheered, a chorus of chittering, and there was an additional sound of movement that Becky thought was Millie relocating up to the bed to attend to Chad. When he finished roaring and started murmuring, she knew her speculation was correct.

She swallowed again, just to see if he'd make the same noise. He did—maybe not quite so loud the second time—but she still felt quite proud of herself.

Next, she hummed. Wings loved the humming—she'd hummed with Wings in her throat for a minute at a time, with the creature squealing, wings vibrating as it crouched on the footboard. Apparently Chad loved it too, if the way he moaned and cried out her name was any indication. But it didn't get the kind of loud appreciation that the swallowing had got her, so she stopped after several seconds.

Becky was having a good time, and she could tell that Chad was, too. By this point he was crying softly, and his legs were trembling. It was time for him to come, and Becky thought she knew how to push him over the edge. Her hands, still gripping his hips, drifted further up and back, until the fingers of both hands met each other inside the crack of his ass. It only took a moment of exploring for her to find the pucker of his asshole. When she did, he whined and thrust into her mouth. It was the first time he'd moved since she started, and she grumbled her discontent. He stopped moving immediately, but kept whining into his arms. Apparently her grumbling felt good, too.

Finally, Becky suckled; she pretended he was a popsicle in the summer sun, and she had to suck all the liquid off just to keep up with the melt. At the same time she stroked the tips of her fingers against his furled muscle—not pressing hard, but a gentle caress, a tease of his hole.

Those two things did the trick, and Chad raised his head and released a very loud and heartfelt, "FUCK!" Becky's heart filled with fondness and pride as his warm cum filled the back of her throat. She held still, and so did he, and after three hearty spurts he was done; she smiled around his dick and finally pulled her mouth down and down and off.

But she wasn't quite finished. Instead of swallowing his cum, she pushed it up into her mouth, lowered herself to lie back on the ground, and then spat it out so it coated her lips and dripped down her chin and her cheeks. The beetles and ant were delighted, and gathered around her head to drink up a sweet snack. Wings and Millie chirped their support.

"Fuck, sweetheart," Chad said, when he finally stood up and took a look himself. "I feel like that should be kind of gross, bugs eating my cum off your face, but it's really hot."

Becky laughed. "I think it's hot, too. And delicious. Darling sweeties." She pet the creatures on their hard, shiny backs until they were done and she was free to sit up. Chad helped her to stand, kissed her and licked off the remnants of his cum, and together they crawled back into bed and snuggled under the blanket. One of the bugs turned off the lamp, and they chittered a goodnight before scuttling out of the room and down the stairs to their abode through the crack in the basement wall.

"That was amazing, sweetheart, just amazing," Chad confessed quietly into Becky's hair.

"It was, wasn't it," she replied, preening at his praise. She could tell Chad was wondering how on earth she'd learned to do that; she'd given him plenty of blowjobs but the last time they'd tried deepthroating she'd gagged so violently that Chad had insisted that they stop, and they hadn't tried again since.

She was half asleep when he finally asked the question.

"Sweetheart, how did you learn how to do that? Have you been practicing? Training?" The strain in his voice implied that he was thinking about exactly how she might have been practicing, and he probably wasn't far from the truth.

"Let's just say that both Wings and Millie have been very helpful over the past couple of weeks."

Chad pulled her closer, his breath hot on her neck. "Are you telling me that you deepthroated Wings?"

She hummed, snuggling into his chest. "I sure did. I deepthroated Wings a lot."

"Oh, fuck. I would like to see that."

"I think that could be arranged."

Chapter Eighteen

SEVEN INCHES OF SILICONE were hilted in Chad's ass and Becky's tits were glistening with sweat. She'd been fucking him for a good ten minutes and he thought he was just about ready to come; all he needed was a little push, a bit of extra attention on the inside or the outside. Either one would do. But she wasn't quite ready for that.

They were using the double-ended dildo tonight, so she had a bit of silicone too, positioned just perfectly to rub against her G-spot with every stroke. She'd also fitted a vibrating ring around the base of the dildo, and that was pressed up against her clit. Becky was fucking herself as much as she was fucking Chad, and he could tell from the blissful expression on her face that she was as close to release as he was.

Becky wasn't going to give him his until she got hers, but Chad was okay with that. He knew it would be worth it when he finally came. So he laid there on his back and did his best to relax. He watched her flushed and shiny tits bouncing in rhythm to her vigorous thrusts and their accompanying grunts and moans. Her hands were on his thighs, pushing his knees up towards his chest, opening him up to her completely. It felt delicious, being fucked so beautifully by the woman he loved. He remembered the first time they tried this, how tentative she'd been, how brave. They had grown so much together over the years.

When Becky's eyes fluttered closed and she lifted her chin up and bit her lip, she looked so exquisite that Chad was pretty sure he was going to come without the usual push. But still, he held on like a good boy. She'd told him he was good, when she'd licked the tip of his dick and worked him with her fingers and eased the end of the dildo into his ass. She'd told him he was a *good boy, such a good boy*, and he desperately wanted to prove to her that he was good. So Chad held back his orgasm, tightened up all his muscles to hold it in and keep it controlled, and waited. Becky fucked herself and fucked him in the process, her head lolled back and whimpering cries escaped her throat, and he watched her and took everything she gave him.

He was so entranced by her that it took him a moment to realize that they had company. Millie was there, climbing up the side of the bed, and it was very curious about what was going on. Millie had watched Chad and Becky fucking before, in all sorts of positions, but it had never seen Becky use the dildo on him.

"Hey, Millie," Chad murmured to the giant millipede, and it chittered a greeting, but didn't take its little black eyes off of where Becky's dildo thrust steadily in and out of Chad's body.

"You like watching me fuck Chad?" Becky asked the bug, her pupils blown, cheeks very pink and flushed. "I like fucking Chad. You want to fuck him, too?"

Millie chirruped, and made a move for Chad's dick, but he lifted up his hand and gently pushed it away.

"Not now, Mill. This is Becky's turn. You can watch, though." It squeaked and withdrew, curling up next to Chad's hip where it could continue to watch the performance.

They were almost done, though. Chad knew it because Becky's thrusts started to stutter, her grunts increasing in heat and volume, growing into cries. He gripped his hands in the sheet, and a moment later Becky cried out, a roar of victorious pleasure, and pulled the dildo out until only the head of it remained, pressing against Chad's prostate. She rotated her hips carefully, rubbing the smooth, hard silicone firmly against that bundle of nerves that held the key to his pleasure.

Chad roared then, too, as he swiftly reached the point of orgasm and zoomed past it, and streams of hot cum spurted out of his dick, covering his stomach and chest.

Millie had not been expecting that, and it flipped its shit, wiggling around on the bedspread and squealing before hopping up and helping itself to the creamy liquid that coated Chad's torso.

Becky and Chad laughed, and she slowly pulled the dildo out of his ass, then unbuckled the harness and pulled it out of her as well. Its loss had Chad feeling empty, bereft, but he took pleasure in watching Becky help Millie clean him up, using a damp cloth instead of her tongue. Chad thought that was a shame, a waste of good cum, but considering she'd just made him come untouched he wasn't going to complain.

After they both had a drink of water and were tucked into bed, Millie curled comfortably next to Chad's head, Becky had an idea.

"You know, Chad," she said slowly, walking her fingers up his chest, "Millie has such a great mouth, but it doesn't have sufficient equipment to fuck your ass. That's quite a shame, don't you think?"

He hadn't really thought about it. He did love fucking Millie's mouth—it was incredible at sucking dick—and they'd played with its ... whatever it was Millie laid its eggs through, but the tube was very short and just wasn't satisfying. But now that he was thinking about it, it was a shame, quite a shame.

"Yeah, it is," he finally answered. "It is a shame."

"Maybe we could do something about that." Becky's smile was mischievous, and she pressed her lips together and raised her eyebrows at him.

"Like what?" He asked, pretty sure he knew exactly what she was going to suggest.

"Well, we've been talking about getting a new dildo. You know, a special one. But what if we also got a new harness? One made especially for Millie?"

Chad looked over at the aforementioned bug, snoozing happily on the pillow next to him. Getting fucked in the ass by Millie would be interesting. He wondered if she could even thrust, or if she'd have to come up with some other movement to make it work. He wanted to find out, and he was absolutely certain Millie was up for it.

"Yeah, that would be cool," he said. "That would be very cool indeed."

"I'll start the process tomorrow, then. I love you."

"I love you too, sweetheart."

Becky grinned, gave him a kiss, and turned over to sleep. He wrapped himself around her, big spoon to her little, and eventually he fell asleep, too.

Chapter Nineteen

CHAD WAS TRYING TO focus on several things at once and he wasn't doing a particularly good job. He was mixing a bowl of goo in the kitchen sink, and he was watching the timer carefully because he only had a limited amount of time before the goo would start to set. It wasn't difficult but he kept getting distracted by the winged bug that was fucking his ass.

The bug was taking that responsibility very seriously.

Chad was bent at the waist and had to keep resting his forehead against the edge of the sink to take deep breaths before getting back to the goo.

The other distraction was even worse: Becky was on her knees, on the floor behind him, and two of the bugs were with her. He'd watched them earlier, as he poured the powder into the bowl and turned on the tap to allow the water to warm up. They had been getting situated then, only a few minutes ago—it felt like *forever* ago—and although he couldn't see them he knew exactly what they were doing. Becky had one bug under her, gripping the front of her torso, and another one on her back. The one on top was fucking her ass and the one on the bottom was fucking her pussy, and watching them both penetrate her while she writhed and moaned and he was standing at the sink waiting for the goddamned tap water to warm up... well, it had been incredibly frustrating. Chad knew that double penetration was one of Becky's favorite treats, whether with human dicks or a dildo or any part of a bug—anything she could shove in there, basically, she'd happily take it—and she was being very vocal about her appreciation at the moment.

The worst part of that particular situation for Chad was that, because he was stuck at the sink and a bit tied up himself, he couldn't see her. He could hear her though, moaning and crying, swearing and encouraging the bugs, which squelched noisily in her wet pussy and her slick ass. They were noisy too, chittering to each other, occasionally squealing, and the one on her back kept vibrating its wings moving the air about the room like a giant fan. The air carried the scent of their fucking, the sweetness of Becky's pussy and the tang of the bugs' natural aroma, and those things combined in a way that went straight to Chad's dick.

It was all very distracting. Frustrating, and distracting.

Since Chad couldn't see Becky he had to imagine it. Her forehead pressed against the cool linoleum, ass in the air, the tapered backends of the two creatures thrusting into her holes, puddles of juice and fluid wetting the ground beneath them. The thought wasn't quite enough to distract him from the sensation of the bug behind him, although it had just slowed its thrusts a bit and was being more spare with its movements. It was, however, focusing them more, concentrating the delicate tip of its backend on the bundle of nerves that all the bugs knew could always be counted on to make Chad cry out in pleasure.

Chad cried out in pleasure and dropped the spoon, which fell into the goo and disappeared, only the silver tip peeking out at the edge of the bowl.

"Dammit!" Chad shouted, his annoyance warring with the pleasant warmth that flooded him below his waist. "You're supposed to be helping me stay hard, not making me come." The bug in his ass squeaked apologetically, but didn't stop.

From the floor behind him came a soft laugh and accompanying amused chirrups, and that annoyed Chad too.

"You're no help either, all I can think about is how you guys look over there, but I can't even see you and you're just distracting me from this..." having finally pulled the spoon completely out of the goo, he dropped it in the sink and sighed. "Whatever."

"Baby, I bet the stuff is ready now, just pour it in the tube and get it over with." Becky paused to moan, a long, low thing, and her knees scuffed against the floor. Chad imagined her legs spreading even more, opening herself to the thrusts as deeply as she could take them. The bugs trilled, and it sounded to Chad as though they were giggling with pride. "Then you guys can join us over here, I'm sure we can think of something we can do with five of us."

Chad was sure of it too, and several options jumped to mind, many of which involved Chad shoving his dick as far down Becky's throat as he possibly could, and weeping as she swallowed around it. Another distraction. He swore as he straightened up as much as he could—difficult, considering the giant bug in his ass—and poured the goo into the long plastic tube that stood upright on the counter.

They'd paid extra for the ultimate version, which took a cast of the balls as well as the dick, so the tube widened at the top on one side.

Chad turned the tube so the wide part (in his head he'd been calling it the ball shelf) faced him and peered down into the tube. The goo didn't completely fill it, but as Chad leaned back over and pulled the tube onto his erect dick, it displaced the goo and the tube overflowed, dripping the viscous, cloudy stuff onto the floor.

"Oh, wow," Becky murmured behind him. "That actually looks really hot. I've never wanted to be a tube full of snot before but I gotta say I'm feeling a little jealous."

The goo embracing his cock felt better than he was expecting, it was warm and seemed almost to penetrate him, covering every centimeter of bare skin.

"Feels good. Just have to do this for a minute or two and then I can pull out and put my cum in your throat. Is it okay if I jizz in your throat, babe?"

She laughed again, that same low and breathy laugh that told him exactly how turned on she was, how close to orgasm.

"Of course, baby. We can all come together, make a big fucking mess all over everything. Cum and eggs and puddles of liquid, slipping and sliding across the kitchen floor..."

"Fuck, Becky, shut up or I'm gonna come in this fucking tube. I don't want to have to use the spare kit."

"You sure don't. I'm planning to send the spare one to your brother. Maybe he can share it with that nice man he's been dating."

Thinking about his brother Brock making a cast of his dick while his very attractive boyfriend fucked him or spanked him or made him suck his dick or whatever they got up to was almost too much for Chad to bear, but by that time the goo had set. It wasn't until then that he realized he had to soften up a bit to pull out, so he reached around behind his back and encouraged the bug to pull out. He thought about the last time he saw the disembodied head of Bradford Bates, and his dick deflated just enough for him to pull out of the tube.

By the time Chad washed himself off he was rock hard again, and Becky was practically screaming into the floor, her two bugs working themselves into a frenzy as they thrust and whistled and vibrated around her. His own bug had slipped back into his asshole while he was washing his hands, and had gone back to focusing on his prostate, which was fine with Chad. He shuffled across the floor to Becky and helped her to kneel. She came up with her eyes closed and her mouth open, and he slipped his dick right into her mouth and all the way back into her throat. With her and Brock and bugs on his mind, the sensation of Becky's mouth around his dick, soft and hot and welcoming, Chad came almost immediately. Becky coughed as his cum shot into her throat, but that didn't stop her from coming too, moaning around his dick and sucking it through her orgasm. The bugs took this as their cue, and all three of them let out ear-shattering squeals and dropped their eggs on the floor, surrounding them all with a great pool of liquid and slimy spheres.

When they were done Chad collapsed on the floor, and the bugs munched the eggs while Chad and Becky cuddled in the rapidly cooling puddle of egg juice.

Chad pulled Becky close and gave her a kiss on the top of her head.

"So you're planning to send that other one to Brock, huh?"

"Yeah, I thought him and his boyfriend might appreciate it. Give them a little activity to do together. You know, a bonding experience."

Chad had to laugh. "You're such an altruist."

"I can be nice." Becky yawned. "So what's next for you?"

"Next, I mix up the silicone and make the thing. What's next for you?"

She bit her lip. "Next, I take a shower and then I go out to the garage and pull out my old leatherworking tools."

"That sounds good to me!" Chad squeezed her, excited. "I'll join you for that shower."

Chapter Twenty

BY THE FOLLOWING AFTERNOON the dildo—a perfect silicone replica of Chad's erect dick, in a shiny, almost metallic black—was ready to be broken in.

Becky could tell that Chad was fascinated by it because he had trouble putting it down. Ever since he'd broken it out of the mold that morning he'd had it either in his hands or close by, and he would stroke it or stare at it when he thought she wasn't looking.

She had to admit it was very impressive. Chad's dick was impressive—her favorite, if she was forced to choose—and she supposed it was different to see a physical piece of yourself out of its usual context and separated from your body; a bit like running into your yoga teacher at the grocery store. It was kind of cute, really. She knew that he was sizing it up, trying to decide if he could take it. While he'd been molding the dildo, she'd been building a harness for Millie. Chad was going to get fucked in the ass with that dildo, and he wasn't sure he was going to be able to make it fit.

"You're being very silly, you know," Becky said, slipping the dildo through the ring on the custom harness to make sure one last time that it would fit. "Your dick is almost exactly the same size and shape

111

as Brock's and he's fucked you so many times. It'll fit, and it won't hurt. In fact, I would bet you money that it will feel *amazing*."

Chad watched her stroke the phallus and check the harness straps. She hadn't had a chance to measure Millie so they had cut the leather from memory. They hoped the straps were long enough to pass around its body, and that they would deal effectively with its undulations. Becky had purchased the leather especially for Millie. Like the dildo it was black, with a slight metallic sheen, and they agreed it should match Millie's own coloring and patina almost perfectly.

Hopefully Millie would come upstairs soon. They'd seen other bugs over the previous twenty-four hours; there had been the mold-making soiree in the kitchen the previous afternoon, of course. Later, the silver moth had kept Becky company in the garage that evening and the following morning as she'd measured and cut the leather and finally sewed the harness together, and it had seemed very keen with the undertaking.

Finally, a couple of ants and beetles had joined Chad as he'd poured the silicone into the mold and then broken it out; he insisted that their fascination with the dildo could not be overstated, although he'd refused to let them touch it (they touched him, instead, and that was just fine).

They knew that the bugs had some kind of group communication, that the knowledge of a single bug was very soon known by all of them. They had no idea how this happened, and didn't really care, but they were counting on this group communication to alert Millie that there was something interesting going on, and they were hopeful that it would show up sooner or later; Chad and Becky were both eager to present it with their gift.

They didn't have long to wait. They were in the bedroom, side by side on the bed, wearing only their underwear. Becky was reading a paperback romance she'd checked out from the public library, and Chad was scrolling through Instagram, when the familiar skittering of Millie's hard little feet against the wood of the stairs drew their attention. A moment later the giant millipede rippled into the room, flowing across the floor and then up to join them on the bed.

"Hey, Millie," Chad greeted her with a pat on the head, and Becky reached behind the pillow for the gift bag. "We have a little something for you. Would you like it?"

Millie would. The creature wiggled and squirmed between them for a moment before it stilled and waited, its antennae twitching excitedly.

When Becky pulled the dildo out of the bag, Millie went a bit wild again, climbing over both of them and the bed, her feet scritching against their skin, before returning to her spot. Becky and Chad both laughed—it seemed to understand what the gift was, and it was excited for it, which was gratifying considering the amount of time and energy they'd spent on it. Becky set the dildo on the bed and reached into the bag a second time, pulling out the harness.

It was a little rough—it had been a while since Becky had done any leatherworking, and the pieces didn't square up at every edge and the stitching was a bit uneven, but the construction was solid. Her only concern was whether or not she got the measurements correct; if it was too tight or the straps were too far apart, it wouldn't work and she would have to go back and try again.

Once again Millie took a moment to caper around the bed before returning to Becky. It stretched up the headboard and curved its back to expose its belly.

"I guess Millie knows what's up," Chad said with a laugh, reaching for the bottle of lube on the bedside table while Becky threaded the dildo into the ring on the front of the harness. Millie stood, unmoving, and squeaked contentedly as Becky wrapped the harness around its body, figuring out the best places to wrap the straps both for stability and for the bug's comfort. Meanwhile Chad slipped off his boxers and started prepping his ass.

By the time Becky was satisfied with the harness Chad was flat on his back, holding his knee back with his left hand and two well-lubed fingers deep inside with his right.

"That looks real good, baby," she murmured, scooting down to lie next to him. Millie skittered to his other side, the black dildo catching on the top blanket a few times and holding her up. But eventually she stopped next to Chad's hip, and watched him press his fingers inside himself and slowly open them like scissors to stretch his tight ring of muscle.

"Millie likes it too," Becky added, as Millie reached out an antenna to gently poke around where Chad's fingers plunged into his asshole. A drop of precum rolled off of the tip of his dick and dropped into his belly button. He didn't seem to notice but Millie squeaked and Becky caught her breath. Becky had a deep and abiding appreciation for Chad's dripping dick.

Chad was going to get pegged by a giant millipede using a dildo made from his own dick, and Becky was going to get to watch. She pressed her thighs together to encourage the warm pressure building there.

Chad noticed.

"Do you want to fuck too, sweetheart?" He asked, pulling out his fingers and wiping them on the towel that was laid under his butt. "I can multitask."

Becky considered it as she rubbed lube up and down the expanse of the dildo. She did want to watch, and if she participated she might not be able to see much. But then Chad laid back down and pulled his knees up, exposing his pink, shiny asshole, relaxed and very slightly open, and his cock lay on his stomach, stiff and purple, and Becky decided she wanted to participate after all.

Becky tore off her bra and panties as Millie chittered and climbed between Chad's legs and up his body. Becky was pleased with how she'd positioned the harness; it was just at the height where the top of Millie's head touched his chin. They both helped the creature line up the head of the dildo with Chad's hole, and he gasped as the millipede gently eased the large, round tip of it through that ring of muscle. It paused there and looked down at him expectantly.

"It's good, Mill," Chad murmured, his cheeks and chest flushed pink. "Real good. Give me more, please." It did as he asked, pressing the dildo into him inch by inch, and eventually it was fully hilted. The process fascinated Becky, and turned her on—she slipped a finger between her legs as she watched the clone of her boyfriend's dick disappear inside his own ass. Eventually Millie stopped, although its little feet continued to move, making little scratches in two lines up Chad's torso. He wiggled slightly, as though it tickled.

"Hey, baby," Becky murmured, circling the finger around her clit and enjoying the sensation of her pussy slicking up. "How does it feel?"

"Feels good, fucking good," he grunted, rubbing his hands up and down Millie's back while it rubbed it's face against his chest and squeaked quietly. "Want you now, your pussy on my dick. Wanna fuck you both at once"

Why not? A drop of liquid dripped down the inside of Becky's thigh, and she didn't want to disappoint him, so together they lifted Millie up and Becky held her on her back as she straddled Chad's torso and lined herself up, then impaled herself on his dick. She was so wet he slipped right in; she moaned and rotated her hips; he was so thick and hot, and it felt so good to have him inside her. Millie undulated her legs, which tickled a little against Becky's back, but the tickle felt good.. Millie squeaked; she thought it felt good, too.

They sat like that for a moment, until Chad began to whine and wiggle, his fingers gripping hard around Becky's hips.

"I think it's time for us to fuck him, what do you think?" Becky asked over her shoulder.

Millie shook her head and chittered, and then she started to thrust.

Becky couldn't see what Millie was doing, but the millipede's legs scratched against her back and she could watch Chad's face, and that was almost as good as watching. His lips were pursed, eyebrows drawn together; she kissed his flushed cheeks, one and then the other, and enjoyed his warm breath against her face. She could feel Millie move as she pressed the dildo into Chad's body and then pulled it back out again, once and twice and then more times, speeding up just a little bit each time, until she reached a pace that made Chad cry out. Millie's movements made Chad's dick move slightly inside Becky, which was

116

helpful since she didn't want to move herself. She did her best to remain still; she was afraid that if she rode him properly he would come, and what would be the fun in that?

So instead she wrapped her arms around his shoulders and embraced his dick in her warm wetness, enjoying the fullness and his noises and Millie's legs against her body and Chad, writhing and moaning and crying out under them.

Once Chad started crying, sweet tears leaking from his eyelids and tracing tracks down his cheeks, Millie got serious. Becky could tell from how Chad's breathing changed that she pulled out the dildo until only the tip remained, and then with steady movements angled slightly up she placed that solid black smoothness against Chad's prostate and rubbed.

Chad seized up and started to yell, and Becky figured that this was her moment. She pressed her knees in, took a breath, and lifted her hips up until only the head of Chad's dick remained inside. Then she rotated her hips, made two tiny thrusts, and then very quickly lowered them to take him all back in again. The sudden filling of her pussy felt amazing, so she did it again—long thrusts coupled with a dance on the tip, at the same time that Millie was attending to his prostate with the dildo. Millie held Becky and Becky held Chad as they worked him together.

Becky thought Chad's dick felt wonderful, sliding through her tight channel, rubbing against every nerve, and she felt herself getting closer and closer to orgasm—but with the two of them working him together, Chad didn't stand a chance.

He came with a bellow, and gripped Becky's hips with white knuckles, holding her down as his dick filled her with cum. It felt good for her too but it wasn't enough to bring her to orgasm, and she whined even as she enjoyed his release. Millie chittered excitedly, clearly proud at having made Chad come via pegging. When Chad was done he lifted Becky and tossed her off; she bounced on the bed beside him and immediately got to work finishing herself off with her fingers. The cum leaking out of her made things a bit more slick than she would have liked, but she had been so close to orgasm and she was desperate to finish. Millie fell onto Chad and he gave her a hug; Millie pulled out the rest of the way and scratched at the harness with her feet, as though trying to take it off. Chad quickly helped her with that, before rolling over and pushing Becky's hand away from her pussy.

"I was so close!" She wailed, but he just grunted and pushed her further up the mattress before spreading her legs wide, crawling between them, and wrapping his lips around her clit. That, paired with two fingers pressed inside her, had her crying out with pleasure and gripping the sheets in her fists. Chad worked her through it, and as it wound down Millie patted her cheeks tenderly with her antennae.

Becky and Chad took a quick shower and when they got back Milie had curled up at the foot of the bed like a strange kind of dog; the dildo, which they'd left lying on the towel and which hadn't yet been washed, she gripped in the legs closest to her head.

"Hey, come on Millie! At least let me have it so we can wash it off." Millie gave it up, grudgingly, and Chad took it to the bathroom. Becky listened to the running water in the bathroom as she tucked herself under the covers.

Once she was under the blanket Becky nudged the giant millipede with her toe, and decided that comparing the sentient bugs they fucked to pets was a bit gross. They weren't like pets at all. They took care of themselves, and they'd taken care of her and Chad too; they were like people, really. Only they were bugs.

By the time Chad came back Millie was asleep, so he kept the dildo and rested it on the pillow between him and Becky.

"You have a nice dick," Becky said sleepily.

Chad nodded. "I'm pretty fond of it."

"Me too. And Millie. Millie's fond of it too."

"Everybody loves my dick," Chad giggled.

"Oh, I have to remember to send the other kit to Brock tomorrow. Do you think he'll bring his dick dildo with him the next time he comes to visit?"

Chad hummed. "I sure hope so. Ask him to."

Becky sighed and huddled down into the blankets, and a few minutes later all three of them were asleep.

Chapter Twenty-One

BECKY ENJOYED ANAL SEX. There was just something about having her ass full of dick or bug and a vibe or some fingers on her clit that pushed her over the edge in just the right way. She enjoyed the ritual, too, the physical and mental preparation that led up to the event itself.

Even though she loved it, the thought of it always made her a little anxious. Her first time had been with Brock, perched on a sink in a dirty bathroom while they were both on the clock, and although he'd made her come it had been a less than ideal way to lose her anal virginity. That experience stayed with her, even years later, and Chad had come up with their ritual to help make her comfortable. She'd have a drink or two to help her relax, and Chad would lube up his fingers and hold her on the bed as he gently worked her ass open. She had control of the vibe, and with that plus lots of patience and kisses and sweet words eventually Chad would ease himself in and then everything would be fine.

Better than fine. Eventually she'd be babbling incoherently, her body wound far past the point where it would usually release an orgasm, juice dripping out her pussy and running down her thighs or dribbling down her ass to join the lube as Chad, or whoever, thrust into her, depending on whether she was on her back or on her knees.

This night she was on her knees, face in a pillow. Chad was behind her, draped over her, his breath hot against her neck. He'd been pounding her up until a minute before this moment, but since she started babbling he'd slowed down his thrusts, made them longer and deeper, and he grabbed the vibe remote out of her hand and turned the speed down to 3. She still pressed the vibe against her clit with as much pressure as she could, even rubbing it against herself in an attempt to give herself just a bit more, but it wasn't enough.

None of it was quite enough, and Chad knew it. He reveled in it. She wanted to cry, or maybe hit him.

"How does it feel? Are you getting close? I'm giving you all I can, you know." Chad murmured and tucked a loose lock of hair behind her ear. The amusement in his voice was palpable.

"You are *not*," she grumbled, and arched her back, pushing herself against him. He moaned in appreciation and pressed a kiss against her shoulder. She wanted to make a grab for the remote, but she wasn't even sure where it was any more. "You're holding back on me. You're a *monster*."

He laughed darkly. "Yes I am," he said, and his admission just annoyed her more.

"*Please*, Chad," she whined, hating the way she sounded but knowing that if she wanted to get off that begging was probably the way to go. "Please, let me come, I'm so close."

He hummed, a thoughtful kind of noise, and then gripped her chin and lifted her head up, aiming it towards the door to the room.

"I don't know, sweetheart," he crooned, "do we have room for one more first?"

Wings crouched in the doorway, its emerald wings spread wide, its thick, curved backend dripping large droplets of clear fluid on the wooden floor.

"Yes," Becky answered, not even having to think about it. "Yes, *please*. How do you want to do it?"

"Good girl," he whispered. "I'm going to pull out for a minute and we're going to rearrange ourselves to be a bit more, ah, bug friendly. Okay?"

She moaned when he pulled out. She was cold, cold and empty without his warm body behind her, without his dick inside her body. He lifted her up and she followed his lead, and in just a minute he was on his back, knees bent, and she was straddling him, leaning against his thighs and shuddering with pleasure as his dick slipped back into her ass. He grabbed her ankles and lifted her feet off the mattress, spreading her knees wider in the process. Then, with a grin, he looked over where Wings still lurked in the doorway, and gestured with his head for the creature to join them.

Wasting no time, Wings took to flight—a rare occurrence—and in a few seconds it had landed next to them and was examining the situation, as though it was trying to figure out what exactly was going on. After not very long at all, the gaze of its shining compound eyes had become fixated on the opening of Becky's pussy, which was very pink and leaking juice down onto Chad's stomach.

"Hop on, Wings," Chad drawled, thrusting up into Becky and making her squeak. "There's room for one more."

Wings didn't need to be asked twice. It tilted its head and looked at Becky first, but when she nodded and nudged her hips forward Wings climbed onto Chad's torso and then up onto Becky's belly. Becky watched as it carefully placed the narrow tip of its backside at her entrance and then gently pushed it in.

"How does it look, sweetheart?" Chad asked breathily. He was gazing at her face, his eyes wide, cheeks flushed with a rosy glow.

"Looks good," she replied. She wanted to tell him more—how slick Wings was, how the tip of it was narrow but it widened so quickly, stretching her pussy around it and filling her up more than she would have thought possible—but she was having trouble forming words. "Feels good."

"I can feel it," Chad whispered a moment later, after Becky had gasped and Wings paused its steady penetration. "I can feel Wings in you."

"*Fuck*," Becky said, because it was all she could manage to say. Her head was light, and she had to close her eyes and lean her head back. Having her sweet Chad and her sweet Wings inside her at the same time was almost more than she could bear.

There were a few words that Becky and Chad knew the bugs understood, beyond a doubt, and *fuck* was one of them. Wings seemed to take Becky's declaration as a suggestion, and it pulled its body almost completely out and then thrust it back in, taking care to rub its tip over her G-spot with both passes. The move made her tremble and holler, and Wings took that as a good sign and did it again, and again, stroking her G-spot each time.

For his part, Chad mostly watched. Becky didn't think he could see much—mostly Wings's back and, well, wings—but he watched her face with those wide, brown eyes, lips slightly parted. He held her feet steady even though she was really starting to wiggle around. After a while she realized that he was also breathing along with her, sucking air into his lungs every time she moaned or cried out, and that although he wasn't thrusting into her he was moving along with her. Every time she shifted her hips to take more of Wings or thrust against it, he moved his hips as well, to remind her that his dick was there. As though she could forget.

Somewhere along the way she'd misplaced the vibrator and she'd been neglecting her clit, choosing instead to reach her hands behind her and grip Chad by the ankles. It didn't matter, though, because she was pretty sure she was going to come anyway. With Chad's dick filling her ass and Wings filling her pussy as it attended so sweetly to her G-spot it was only a matter of time.

Eventually the time did come, and so did Becky. When the orgasm began to crest she took a chance and bore down. The chance was worth it—she squirted, soaking herself and Wings and her sweet and patient boyfriend with a substantial amount of warm fluid. All three of them shrieked, and Wings shook its wings, spraying wet droplets all over the bed before pulling out and squealing again as it dropped a clutch of eggs right onto Chad's stomach. That freed up Becky to move, and she shook her feet free of Chad's hands and set them on either side of his hips, and rode his dick until he came, too. It didn't take long. She delighted in the flush that spread down his chest and the way he bared his teeth as he worked through the end of it.

While Becky worked to finish off Chad, Wings cleaned up the eggs, finally settling next to Chad's head. It patted his hair and squealed along with him when he came. When Chad was finished he pulled

Becky down into an embrace, and Wings petted them both, and they snuggled together until they all fell asleep.

Chapter Twenty-Two

THE HARD ONE COMES to us. It comes to us through the crack that separates our abodes, and it falls to its knees and asks us, begs us, so we take it. We strip it to its skin and our mistress binds it, wraps it in webs and hangs it above the floor. We take turns with it, and it gives us its *yes*, so we do what we wish, as long as it continues to give us its *yes*.

We know that in time the soft one will come for it, take it back to their abode, so we will enjoy it for as long as we can.

We need it.

It was Saturday afternoon. Chad had gone to work that morning, a rare Saturday workday, required to meet a deadline. The disappearance of Bradford Bates had made the news, although the police never made any connection between the disappearance and Chad and Becky.

Unfortunately, it had also left their company understaffed, which meant more work for everyone until he could be replaced.

Becky had just been to the grocery store. She came home with the chest in the back of her truck filled with half a dozen canvas sacks full of cans and jars, and there were a couple of insulated bags in the front seat filled with ice cream and produce. She was relieved to see Chad's car was in the drive, but when she yelled for him to come and help her carry in the groceries, he didn't respond.

Becky grumbled as she carried the groceries inside by herself. She was annoyed partially because she had to make two trips, and partially because she was pretty sure she knew where he was. He wasn't ignoring her. He'd been annoyed that morning about having to go in to work on his day off, and had snapped at her twice as he was getting ready to leave. They both knew he was being unfair, taking things out on Becky instead of directing it towards work. He had made a sincere apology before he walked out the door, but still, it had stung.

When Chad got frustrated it could go one of two ways, and since he hadn't tackled her on her way in the door, to hold her down and rip her clothes off, she figured that today it was going the other way.

She crept upstairs first, but the bed was empty and cold, so she headed into the basement. She took her phone, turned on the flashlight, and started recording as she stepped through the crack in the wall and into the dark, cool cavern beyond.

It was dark, but it was not quiet. As Becky made her way down the stone passageway she could hear the shuffling of the horde, accompanied by soft chittering and, as she reached the opening into the cavern, a quiet grunt, followed by another one a few seconds later. The grunts were Chad, and they were sweet. Both her brain and her body were curious to see what they might mean.

Becky shined her light around the room, her phone dutifully recording everything in its sight, and as her brain interpreted what exactly she was seeing, pressure built between her legs and her nipples stiffened under the thin cotton of her tee shirt. She wondered briefly if this was how Chad had felt, weeks before, when he'd come down here and found her strung up, wound up, and begging for release.

That's exactly how he was now, completely covered in spider's webs except for his dick and his ass and his chest and the lower part of his face. The webbing glimmered under the dazzle of her phone's light where it wrapped around his legs and body. His arms were pulled behind his back, thick ropes leading from his knees and sides and shoulders to the stalactites and stalagmites that dotted the cavern floor and ceiling. Giant bugs of all sorts—insects and arthropods, things with wings and others lacking even legs—covered the floor and walls of the space. They wriggled and trilled when her light hit them, and they rubbed against her legs as she walked into the cavern and towards the man who was the focus of everyone's attention. If Chad heard or sensed her, he gave no indication. Aside from his soft grunts, he was completely silent.

Chad was face down, about five feet off the ground, and from where she stood Becky had an excellent view of his backside; legs spread wide, dick long and hard, pointing at the ground. Becky squatted to the ground and angled the phone up to get the best view possible.

Elshob was crouched on a net of web cast just above him. The spider was massive, almost as long as Becky was tall, and it was black and glossy. The creature had her back to Becky, and as Becky watched

Elshob lowered her abdomen and pressed her protrusion into Chad's asshole. He squirmed and moaned and the creature thrust, a sudden, almost violent movement, and Becky was certain she saw the protrusion expand with the passing of an egg from the spider and into the man. He grunted and shook, and the horde vibrated and squeaked as one.

"Chad," Becky murmured from her place under him. His head turned to the side, as though he was searching her out.

"Becky," he whispered. "You're here. You can see."

"Eggs okay?" She asked. "Just making sure." They had a strict "no eggs" policy which the bugs followed... Becky would say *religiously* although she was pretty sure the bugs didn't have a religion, unless their religion involved fucking her and Chad. That policy had only been broken once, although they'd talked about doing it again.

Chad nodded vigorously, hard enough to make his whole body shake.

"I asked for it." His voice was higher than usual, and sounded strained. "Wanted to be hers, for a bit. I hope that's okay. Tough day at work." He sounded apologetic, like it had just occurred to him that he should have asked her permission first.

"It's fine, baby. Sometimes you just need to be tied up and filled with eggs."

She shuffled over to have another look at his backside. Elshob had pulled out and was taking a look too, poking at his ass with one of her front legs. The cheeks of his ass were spread wide apart to expose his puckered hole to the air, and his entire backside was shining. As Becky watched through her phone a stream of clear liquid dribbled out and splashed onto a black beetle on the ground below. From this close

Becky could see that his hole was slightly parted, as though something lay just inside, barely being held in. She considered licking it, standing on her toes and reaching out with the tip of her tongue, pressing it just inside his opening, seeing what the egg tasted like with the ring of his ass tight around her tongue. She didn't, but the thought made her pussy throb with warmth.

"Are you all full?" She whispered, the bugs echoing her with a soft chitter. "One more egg?"

"I am full." He moaned, his head lowering, hanging down, chin not quite reaching his chest. "But I want to try one more. Be with me?"

Becky took one final shot of Chad's dripping ass and Elshob turning on her web to give him one more deposit. She licked the drip of precum from the tip of his dick—he flinched and cried out. The bugs vibrated; Becky giggled before she took the three steps to stand by his head. Although the cavern was chilly Chad's face was flushed, and felt hot under Becky's fingers. She pressed her palm against his right cheek and he leaned into her. A moment later he released a shuddering grunt and then a long, heavy whine, his lower lip turning white under the pressure of his teeth. Her stomach clenched in sympathy. Becky was sure her panties were soaked through. The bugs knew it, too, if the way they pressed closer to her legs was any indication.

Becky waited for Chad's breathing to steady before she spoke again, her fingers stroking down his cheek. She could hear Elshob shuffling on the web above them.

"How are you feeling, baby?"

"Puh... perfect," he finally moaned, raising his head again and turning it from side to side blindly, his jaw relaxed, a trail of drool trickling out the corner of his mouth. She wiped it off with her thumb. "I'm so full."

"I"m so proud of you, Chad, so proud. You took more than you thought you could and you did it. You're so good. I love you."

"I love you, too. I am... good. Go see, Becky, go see how full I am."

She took her time, running her hand across his body within the view of the phone camera as she slowly made her way down. She tweaked his nipples, and rubbed a palm over his distended abdomen. She shivered, remembering how it felt when she was filled with eggs, how they filled her up almost to the point of bursting, and how hard she came around them. She wanted Chad to come like that, and she wanted to get it on her camera when he did.

When Becky reached Chad's backside and shined her camera light on his asshole, she was greeted by the sight of almost half an egg, his ring of muscle stretched thin around it, barely holding it in. The egg was a cloudy white, and fluid dripped lazily around it. Becky, amazed, pressed on it experimentally; Chad shouted and she stopped. Elshob had turned back around and lowered her own face to Chad's backside, so her multiple eyes were close to Becky's face; she was checking out her handiwork too.

"You did an excellent job, Elshob," Becky said, giving the monstrous spider a smile. "What's next?"

Chapter Twenty-Three

CHAD'S SATURDAY AT WORK had been remarkably terrible.

When he arrived at the office the police were there. They had updates on the case and wanted to ask a few more follow-up questions. Chad had done his best, and hadn't given anything away, but it had still been very stressful. And then Sam, Chad's supervisor who had only two weeks left before he would leave for his hot new contract, took Chad to task for code that he'd been writing for weeks. Code that, incidentally, Sam had checked several times before and hadn't found issue with. But he had issues with it *now* and Chad needed to rewrite full sections. And that was stressful, too.

Once he got started it wasn't nearly as much work as he was afraid it would be, and maybe Sam had a point about the code after all. Chad swallowed his pride and told him so on his way out the door. He even remembered to invite him to his and Becky's house for dinner the next weekend, to say goodbye before he left town for good.

When Chad got home he was ready to be taken care of. Becky wasn't there, she was out running errands, and he could text to ask her when she'd be home, or... or he could go into the basement, through the crack in the wall, and he could ask the bugs to take him.

They'd taken Becky before, and she'd looked so good, trussed up in Elshob's web and hanging off the ceiling. She hadn't had to *do* anything but be present; she'd been reduced to her holes, the recipient of whatever the bugs had wanted to give her. And even then they'd cared for her, kept her fed, made sure that she wanted everything they did to her.

He wanted that, too.

So he crept through that dark crack unannounced, lowered himself to his knees in the cool darkness of the cavern, only the shuffling of insectoid legs to let him know anything was even there, and he said *please*.

He only had to ask once. The horde came to him, slowly stripped his clothes, and then coated his skin with that thick, greasy stuff that kept the webbing from sticking too closely to his skin. They were attentive as they spread it on him, their stiff little feet scratching his skin and carding through his hair as they crawled over him, rolling him onto his back and then his stomach to make sure they'd covered him completely. By the time Elshob herself was there wrapping his legs and his arms and his body and finally his head—all but his mouth and nose covered in that glimmering white stickiness—he felt as though he'd been on the edge of orgasm for hours.

Then Elshob slung him over her back and carried him up. With his eyes covered Chad lost his sense of direction, but he could tell they were going up. They reached a place where she was able to set him down again, and for several minutes he could hear the sticky *shuff* as her body produced the thick, tacky threads. She wrapped more around him, concentrating on his hips and shoulders and thighs. Eventually she lifted him up again, holding him tight as she moved around him. For several minutes she moved around him, chirping occasionally in that deep, unearthly voice she had that was so unlike the other bugs. And then, suddenly, she was gone, and Chad was floating. Gravity told him which direction was down—his head was down, and the rest of him was up. His ass was in the air, legs spread wide and his knees pointing to the ground. He could feel his dick, hanging stiff and unsupported in the chilly, damp air of the cavern. It rested against the web that wrapped his torso up to his lower chest, where it suddenly cut off to leave his nipples exposed. He felt vulnerable, but also safe, and as he listened to the trill and squeak of the bugs as they moved about on the stone floor below him he grew more and more excited. A drop of precum dripped from his dick onto the creatures amassed below, and the first of them climbed onto him and eased something into his mouth.

Chad lost track of time. There were so many of them, and they covered him, crawling on his skin and the webbing that bound him, so many legs and feet and wings and so much chittering it was hard to tell exactly how many they were. He'd been expecting them to fuck him, to penetrate his ass and suck his dick and maybe press parts of themselves between his lips and down into his throat, and they did all of these things. So many of them took him, over and over again, stretching and pulling and swallowing him, and he had expected that—but he hadn't expected the number of them that simply climbed on him. They covered him completely, in a way that was oddly non-sexual. Having them close made it easier to handle the pain and frustration when over and over again they worked him almost to the point of release but then refused to let him come.

It made him a little crazy, which is maybe why he made that last request. He just wanted to be theirs, all of theirs, and what better way to give yourself to bugs than to let them lay their eggs in you?

He couldn't remember afterwards what exactly he'd asked for, but they understood. Before he even grasped what was happening the horde was off him and Elshob was shifting him. She moved his head and shoulders up but kept his ass higher, legs spread apart. If he'd been forced to hold his body that way himself it would have been difficult, but because the web held him, because it was *them*, it was easy. All he had to do was exist, and take what they gave him.

Elshob gave him eggs. She'd fucked him before, and had even used an egg as a bit of a teaser, rolling it through the tube that protruded down from her abdomen and dripped fluid on the floor as she skittered heavily from room to room in their house. That tube would slip into his asshole, and then the egg would roll through the tube. It felt good. But she'd never pushed the egg all the way through, because he'd never asked for it before.

The first one was a bit of a shock, even though he'd known it was coming. It felt larger than he'd expected it to, and more firm, but also good. It was a little bit of them, inside his body, and that part of it he liked very much. She gave him a second one, and that was good too, and another. She kept depositing them, checking before each one that he still wanted it, until he was full.

And then, as though in a dream, Becky was there.

"Chad." Her whispered voice was the most beautiful thing Chad had ever heard. He could imagine her there, how her eyes would shine as she took him in, trussed up and helpless, belly swollen with Elshob's eggs.

She checked to make sure he was okay, and his heart nearly burst with affection for her. And then she asked if he was full, if he could take another egg. He could feel the ones that were already inside him pressing to get out; he wasn't sure he could physically fit another one in there but he could tell from the way she asked that she wanted him to say *yes*. So he said *yes*, and Elshob gave him one last egg and he pressed his heated cheek against his girlfriend's cool, soft hand, and he thought that he might die of happiness.

Becky walked down to where Elshob was, to look at the eggs, which must be nearly bursting out of his ass. He thought he was going to burst. Becky murmured, and Elshob chittered, and a pressure at his backside made him shout in pain, and something else. The pressure eased and Chad could breathe again. The eggs pressed inside him, all around him, and his cock felt so heavy and hot in the air of the cave.

"Please," he called out—he tried to yell, although he expected it sounded more like a whisper. "Please, I want to come now."

Becky's fingertips stroked his left ass cheek tenderly, and her lips and nose pressed against the back of his ballsack. He could feel her smile, and her hum, her warm breath as she rubbed her face into his soft skin.

"You smell so good, Chad," she cooed, not addressing his question. "We're almost done, just one more thing. Relax."

With her assistance, he relaxed. Very purposefully, starting with the muscles in his head and working his way down his body, every muscle received the same instruction: *relax*. Becky continued her attentions, her delight with his balls, fingertips gently massaging whatever skin they could reach, except for the skin he wanted her to touch the most. But that didn't matter. By the time she reached his knees, his heartbeat was slow and his muscles were slack. And then, there was a new sensation. At first he wasn't certain he was feeling it at all, but eventually there were enough of them that he was sure.

There were small legs, tiny ones; legs of the size you see on not giant bugs, but regular-sized ones. There were dozens of them—hundreds, maybe—and they were gathering on his dick.

This was new.

"Becky?" He called, although now he could tell his voice was only a whisper. "Becky, what is that?"

"It's spiders, baby." She was back next to his head, her palm against his cheek, cool and protective. "Elshob's little ones."

Chad licked his lips. Both his lips and his tongue were dry; he needed a drink of water.

"What are the spiders doing?"

She hummed. "Do you trust them? Do you trust me?"

"Oh god, yes," he moaned.

She kissed his temple and pressed her forehead against his. "Then wait, and you'll find out."

It tickled; whatever it was that was happening, it tickled, and itched, just a bit. Not just on the outside of his dick, where the little spiders scurried and scampered and climbed over one another, but inside, too. Just at the tip, at first, but as the minutes passed the itchy tickle worked its way further and further down his urethra. It felt... strange. Not bad, exactly. It was interesting. Combined with the fullness of the eggs, however, it was very close to good.

"Oh, shit." That was Becky. She'd moved, so she was next to his shoulder instead of by his head, but her hand still pressed against his cheek.

The tickling continued, down Chad's urethra and then up again, as though his dick was being filled with something. Chad was very sure he knew what it was being filled with and he wanted to ask, he wanted to make sure, but he was afraid that the confirmation would be enough to make him come untouched.

Becky's voice helped to keep him grounded. She hummed and moaned and he could feel her moving around, watching the spider's lay eggs in his dick. That's what was happening, wasn't it? Chad couldn't imagine what else could be happening, and he wanted to see.

"How are you doing, baby?" Becky was back, her breath warm against his ear.

"I'm all full of eggs."

She giggled. "You are. How does it feel?"

"I'm afraid I'm gonna come." He whined in desperation.

"Not yet. You need to be a good boy and wait until I give you permission. Okay?"

Chad could do that. He was good for Elshob and good for Becky and for Brock and Sam and...

That was unexpected. *Sam.* A sudden throb radiating out from his balls had him pushing the thought of his supervisor's cocky smile, dark eyes, and juicy ass out of his mind.

While Chad had been considering this new impression of his supervisor the spiders crawled off of him in waves, and by the time he returned to himself they were all gone. The tickling in his dick remained.

"Okay baby, it's almost time. Just one more thing to do." Becky took a step back. A shuffle above announced the arrival of the mistress, and with the familiar scrape of claws against skin the layer of webbing covering his eyes was off, and Chad could see again.

The light was bright and it took a moment for his eyes to adjust. He saw Becky's face first, close to his. She was smiling; joyful, excited. Her face was awash in the blue glare from the screen of her cell phone. The flashlight was on; that was the light that had blinded him. The light was aimed down his body, and as his eyes followed the beam he found it was aimed, unsurprisingly, at his dick, which was exactly as swollen and purple as he expected it to be. The tip of it was covered with a glistening silver sheen; as he watched a drop formed and slowly detached itself, falling into the darkness below. A soft, rolling chittering was the only indication of the horde that Chad knew surrounded them.

"Woah."

"Yeah," Becky agreed. "Woah."

She extended a finger and touched the silver tip, where another drop was already forming. He shuddered at the sensation, but as she moved the phone shifted and he caught a glimpse of the screen. There was an unmistakable red circle in the center of the bottom of the screen. Stars burst around the edge of his eyes as he held himself back from coming yet again.

"Are you recording this?" His voice sounded high and strained in his head.

"Yeah," she answered nonchalantly, her fingers closing around the head of his dick and giving it a squeeze. "Gonna send it to your brother. Give him a little something to tide him over before his next visit."

Chad lost control of his body completely. His orgasm felt like a punch to the stomach and a kick to the balls at once, with a brick to the head added for good measure. He heard shouts echoing around the cavern before he realized they were coming from him. His dick exploded, or that's what it looked like, felt like; a burst of thick cream, laced with silver, sprayed out, a veritable geyser of cum mixed with tiny silver spider's eggs, and it rained down onto the horde of bugs gathered on the ground below.

That wasn't the only explosion. Chad's orgasm contracted his abdominal muscles even as it relaxed his sphincter, and his body began the process of pushing out the eggs that Elshob had laid in his gut minutes before. They landed heavily, a slow torrent of distinctive *plops* as one egg after another exited his body and fell to the floor. He was shaking too hard to notice the details, his body overwhelmed by the warm pleasure of the ferocious release and the slowly-growing emptiness that somehow heightened the intensity of the orgasm and pushed it to last longer than he would have thought possible.

Chad was aware of Becky laughing, her lips on his face and her arms wrapped around his shoulders, and he could hear the bugs celebrating around them. The ones with wings vibrated, and the air filled with droplets of wet; it felt like being outside in the early morning, the cool air filled with mist, which coated him and which Becky wiped away tenderly from his face and then from her own. He listened as the horde crawled and squealed and noisily chomped at the eggs, clearly telegraphing their joy and pleasure. Chad had done well, and they were pleased, so he was pleased too.

Becky was pleased, and Elshob too. Becky held Chad, whispered praise as Elshob moved mysteriously on the web above him, and

140

slowly, gently, lowered to the ground and unwrapped him. Millie and Wings had towels and blankets which they had brought in from the house; Becky had finally tucked the phone away so the room was pitch dark again, but it was nice because she had both hands free to wipe Chad down and wrap the blanket around him before helping him sit up.

"How are you feeling, baby?"

"Tired. Really hungry."

"But good?"

The concern in her voice struck a chord in his heart; he opened the blanket and pulled her inside with him, a little cocoon just for them.

"Very good. That was a lot and I'm not sure I would do it again, but it was what I needed today."

Becky snuggled against him. Elshob was nearby, Chad could hear her heavy shuffling as she helped some of the others tidy up the last of the detritus from Chad's visit. Most of the horde had already left, crawling through the openings in the back of this cave to the maze of caverns that Chad knew lay behind. Millie pressed her head against his hip and chittered happily when they patted her head, and then she was gone, too. They held each other and moments later they were alone in the darkness.

Chad moved first. "Come on, let's go. I need some food."

"You need a bath," Becky answered, turning on her phone light again.

"I do." Although Becky had done her best with the towel he was still coated by the greasy stuff, and as she stood and shuffled towards the passageway that would lead them to their house he could feel a warm trickle of residual juice drip out of his ass and down the back of his right thigh. He thought about how good it would feel to take a warm bath and have Becky help him clean the rest of the stuff off. Maybe if he asks very nicely she'll wash his hair, and maybe—probably—if she's very good he will give her a reward, too.

Chapter Twenty-Four

"CHAD?"

Becky glanced over at her boyfriend, standing in the kitchen doorway and looking overwhelmed and a bit upset. She couldn't help but notice that he also looked good. His hair was a mess and his cheeks were very pink, his button-up shirt was untucked and she was very sure his jeans were unzipped. He'd gone down to the basement earlier to bring up some lightbulbs—one of the lamps in the living room had gone out and they wanted to replace it before that evening—and when he hadn't come back up immediately Becky figured he'd gotten distracted, maybe met someone down there or even gone through the crack in the wall to find someone to play with. It looked like he'd done that, but maybe he'd gotten more than he bargained for.

When he didn't answer, Becky started to grow concerned. The bugs had never hurt him, either of them, but they were animals—weren't they?—so you could never be *entirely* sure. Could you?

"Chad, baby, are you okay?" She set down the knife and the ginger root she was peeling and stepped quickly across the floor to lay a palm against his cheek.

Finally his eyes settled on her.

"Hey, sweetheart," he murmured, sounding a bit out of focus. "I'm okay. Just, uh..." He pushed his lips together and swallowed.

"They didn't hurt you, did they?"

He reared back, shocked at her suggestion.

"No! No, not at all. I had a real good time, Millie and Eddie tag-teamed me... I mean, Millie took the front and Eddie took the back. I came so hard I couldn't see, I'm surprised you didn't hear me up here, I was yelling pretty loud at the end. No, they were good. It's not that. It's..." He trailed off again and looked at the floor. "Eddie."

"Eddie," Becky repeated, but Chad didn't speak again.

Becky looked at the oven clock and sighed. She didn't like seeing Chad upset like this, but Sam would be arriving soon—in fifteen minutes, if he was on time, and for all his other faults he was usually on time—and she'd only just started preparing dinner. Chad needed a shower, and a fresh set of clothes—his jeans were filthy and his hair full of dust; even Sam would think he looked like he'd spent an hour fucking some bugs in a cave.

She tried once more, this time pushing her fingers into the hair just above his right ear and squeezing it in her fist. It would hurt, just a little sting, and that might be enough to pull out of him whatever he was holding in. He whined and bit his lip, and when she loosened her hold he opened his eyes and spoke.

"Do you remember Thelma?"

Chad's voice was soft but his words were clear enough. Becky frowned.

"You mean my great aunt?"

"No! Noooo. No." He shook his head, scattering dust onto his shoulders. "The praying mantis. You remember? Earl named it 'Thelma' when he was here last month, because it kept trying to eat the broccoli off his plate."

That jogged her memory. Her cousin Earl—second cousin, really, her great aunt Thelma had been his MeeMaw—had come to visit for the first time since they'd moved into their new house. Becky and Earl had grown up close; his sister Gracie had been Becky's best friend for as long as she could remember until her parents moved her to the city when she was in high school, and she'd had a crush on Earl for almost that long. He was tall and broad, with silky dark hair and a beautiful big nose, and those *lips*. He bore a passing resemblance to Chad, which meant he bore one to Brock, too. It wasn't until this most recent visit that Becky realized that the most likely reason she'd been so willing to throw herself into Brock's path like she did was because he reminded her so much of Earl—Earl, who would not so much as hug Becky hello once he found out she had a crush on him when she was in the fourth grade and he was in high school. Brock was nothing like Earl, however, and neither was Chad. Despite his stint in the armed forces Earl was a soft man, sweet and shy, and more than willing to let a giant praying mantis eat broccoli off his plate.

"I remember Thelma," Becky confirmed. "What about her?"

Chad pulled a chair out from the kitchen table with a shaking hand, and sat.

"Well, what do you know about praying mantises? Female ones, I mean."

Becky shrugged.

"I mean, the only thing anybody knows, I guess. Once they're done fucking they eat... OH my GOD, she didn't try to BITE YOUR HEAD OFF, DID SHE?" Becky, frantic, patted her hands around Chad's neck and peered close, looking for any evidence of scratches or bite marks. Chad laughed and waved her off.

"No, nothing like that. Oh my god, she wasn't near me. But I saw..." his eyes lost focus again, "Eddie."

Becky gasped, and was able to pull a chair out for herself to slip into before her legs collapsed under her.

"Eddie," she repeated, tears springing into her eyes. "That horny bug. I figured it would die fucking, someday."

Chad nodded, his mouth pulled into a frown that suggested very strongly he was trying not to cry.

"Eddie had just finished with me, dropped a whole clutch of eggs down my legs—my jeans are pretty damp, they're gonna need a good soak—and Thelma was there watching, and Eddie just hopped right over to her. She was more than happy to take him, so he climbed on her back and he..." Chad sobbed, and Becky took his hand and stroked it consolingly, "he was fuckin' her, you know, just so happy to be fucking, he didn't really care who, you know, and then she just... she just turned around and..." Chad devolved into sobbing. Becky scooted her chair closer and put her arms around him, wiping her own tears on his shoulder.

"He didn't stop, though," Chad mumbled through his tears and wiped his nose on his sleeve. "I'm proud of him. He kept right on going, even after she bit his head off. He was such a sport, you know? Such a good fuck, all the way to the end." He sighed. "Even dropped a whole other clutch of eggs when she was halfway through eating him."

A thoughtful pause. "Actually, never mind, that may just have been perimortem voiding."

"Oh, Chad," she murmured. "I'll miss Eddie for sure, but that's the way bugs are. I guess you can make them big and give them ways to communicate with other species, but at the end of the day they're still bugs. Thelma's still a praying mantis; she's just doing what praying mantises do."

"I guess you're right. And at least I got to be fucked by him one last time before he died."

Chad sighed and Becky reached over to dab his face with her own sleeve. Then she glanced at the oven clock again.

"Chad, I hate to do this, but Sam is going to be here in ten minutes, I need to finish prepping dinner, and you look like you just got fucked by some bugs. So why don't you go upstairs and take a nice hot shower, and we'll talk about a memorial for Eddie tomorrow. Okay?"

Chad agreed, and headed upstairs as Becky returned to the ginger.

Chapter Twenty-Five

TWENTY MINUTES LATER THE sound of the shower upstairs had finally silenced, and Becky was standing in the kitchen next to Chad's supervisor Sam—well, his former supervisor, for the four years or so leading up to Friday.

Sam poured the wine as soon as he was in the door. It was a large bottle of Cabernet, and he insisted it would go great with Thai food. Then he offered to help Becky with the prep, and she moved on to slicing onions and gave Sam ginger duty.

Becky watched him out of the corner of her eye as she did her best to avoid the onion mist and he monologued about his new job. She had asked him about it hoping for a conversation, but she'd forgotten, or maybe blocked out, how self-centered Sam could be. That was okay, really. He was very nice to look at, even though he wasn't her type. He was too short, for one thing, and his smile always seemed to her to be just on the wrong side of genuine. He was certainly handsome, but it was in a way that was simply present as opposed to being striking the way that Chad or Brock or even Earl were striking. He was a little boring, truth be told, but he had a nice body and especially a nice ass.

She'd noticed it for ages, maybe since the first time she'd met him, but she was still a bit surprised when Chad admitted after the bugs had left after playtime on Wednesday night that he'd noticed Sam's ass, too, and that he wouldn't mind getting to know it better.

From that point on it was Operation Seduce Sam. The plan was to get him in bed before the end of the evening (or on the sofa, table, or even floor, they weren't picky). And if the plan crashed and burned it wouldn't matter because it was unlikely they would ever see him again. The bugs had been warned that a guest was coming and they had asked them to stay away although who knows if they would. Becky wasn't too worried about that though; Sam seemed like a pretty open-minded guy.

Sam's voice paused, and Becky turned to him and said "Chad has a crush on you, you know," at the same time that he turned to her and held up a piece of ginger and said "you can use a piece of ginger as a butt plug, you know."

Becky's cheeks heated, and she had the great pleasure of watching a blush bloom across Sam's cheeks.

After a long silence, Sam spoke first.

"Really? He... he told you that?"

Becky shrugged and put on her best *cool* act, although her heart fluttered wildly in her chest.

"Yeah, he told me. He is my boyfriend, after all. We share a lot with each other." She ventured a glance over at him. He was still holding up the piece of ginger, and his cheeks were now crimson. "We share. You understand."

Sam's expression of surprise very quickly relaxed to a crooked, cocky smile that Becky kind of hated but that also made her pussy relax.

"Yeah, I think I understand." The tip of his tongue darted out between his lips, leaving them slightly shiny. Becky pressed her thighs together and he glanced down. He'd noticed—of course he had. He returned his gaze to her face and settled on her lips, and shifted slightly closer to her, returning his attention to the piece of ginger root in his hand.

"So," Becky said, feeling flustered but desperately wanting not to show it. "Do you ever put ginger in your ass?"

"Only Bates," Sam quipped with a grin, and the feeling that hit Becky was a very strange combination of guilt and lust. The thought of Sam being fucked in the ass by Chad's former workplace nemesis was oddly compelling, but the memory of Bates's head on the backs of the beetles, the taste of his flesh on her tongue, made her feel ill.

Sam's face fell when he took in whatever Becky's face had done.

"Oh, no, I'm sorry, bad joke! Bad joke!" He set down the root on the edge of the sink and carefully pulled the knife out of her hand before taking her hands in his and stroking their backs gently with his thumbs. "I'm sorry, Becky, sometimes my mouth just opens and says shit before my brain has time to filter it out. I know you guys weren't fond of him but that was out of line."

Sam's thumbs felt good, and Becky didn't really want him to stop. She'd also had a moment to digest the other part of what he said, and she wanted to investigate that further.

"Did you, um," she began, her breath just a bit more heavy than she'd like, "did you really, uh, with Bates? Or was that just a joke?"

Sam's chuckle was warm against her cheek. When did he get so close?

"Oh yeah, sure. We dated for a while when I first started working there. It was on the down low, because he reported to me, but it didn't last long." A small sigh. "He was a good fuck, though. Sweet little piece of ginger."

Ginger. Becky took a step back and pulled her hands out of Sam's; they were cold and she missed his thumbs. But yet another idea had taken over her brain.

"The ginger."

Sam picked the root up again and held it in front of her eyes.

"This ginger?"

She nodded, feeling brave.

"I wonder how it would feel to have ginger in my ass?"

Sam tried to hide his surprised delight, but Becky was pleased to find that she saw right through it.

"You want it? You're sure?"

She smiled in a way she hoped looked coy.

"Well... maybe both of us? Would you like to do it, too?"

His eyes were shining and she could see his dick, more than halfway hard, pressing against the front of his slacks. He wasn't nearly as large as Chad, she was pretty sure, but he wasn't *small*, and anyway she wasn't too concerned. Becky had been around long enough to know that size mattered less than how you used it, and she was pretty sure that Sam knew how to use it. She pressed her thighs together again, and his grin became just slightly predatory on top of his usual charm.

"Sure," he answered, drawing out the vowel. "I'll do it if you do it." He glanced towards the door and his eyebrows drew together slightly. "Do you think Chad will mind?"

Becky shook her head. "No, he won't mind. To be honest?" She leaned towards him to whisper in his ear, "it'll turn him on. He *loves* ass play."

Sam grinned and bit his lip, turned back to the sink and picked up his paring knife.

"In that case, let's get to it."

Becky took a long sip of the Cabernet—it was good, complex; dry and fruity, and its flavor brought a splash of saliva into her mouth, which she swallowed down along with the wine. She returned to her vegetables—the onions were done, so she moved on to the bell peppers. As she sliced she considered what might happen later. Things were going very well with Sam, and were happening even more quickly than she'd expected it to. If they both got ginger in their asses before dinner, they'd be fucking for dessert. And considering it wasn't even six-thirty yet... they could have a really lovely evening in store for them indeed.

She'd just started to daydream about a horde of beetles joining the three of them in an orgy, when Sam cleared his throat. She glanced over to see that he'd peeled the chunk of ginger and was in the process of sculpting it into a little shape, wider and longer on one end, growing more narrow, and then flaring out again.

"That looks good, Sam. Looks like a cute little butt plug."

He raised an eyebrow and bit his lip again. It was almost annoyingly attractive, and he knew it. His voice when he spoke was noticeably rough.

"You ready to take it, Becky? I can help. Hold you open, slip it in for you."

She plucked the ginger plug from his fingers and gave it a sniff. Sam's pupils dilated visibly and Becky couldn't control her answering gasp. He was standing close again, somehow; his breath smelled like red wine and sex.

"I think you should do it first, Sam. I can hold *you* open, slip it in for you."

To Becky's surprise, Sam didn't argue; he didn't even look surprised. He simply unbuttoned and unzipped his trousers and pulled them down along with his underwear—black silk briefs with a bright orange waistband, which Becky thought were a bold fashion choice—and leaned against the edge of the sink, sticking his butt out and giving her another one of those cocky smiles.

"I'm ready if you are," he said, shaking his rump and using his left hand to pull his left cheek aside to expose himself to the room. Becky's eyes were drawn to it, and she reached over quickly for the bottle of olive oil before she took the couple of steps that separated her from Sam's naked asshole. It was brown, but very clean; she thought he must have taken a shower before coming over, or maybe he had one of those bidet attachments on his toilet at home that she and Chad had been thinking about investing in. His entire ass was completely hairless. It was... kind of weird actually, but she wasn't going to complain. No she wasn't—she was going to stick the piece of ginger right into that hole and they were both going to enjoy it.

Becky took a moment to slick it up with a couple of fingertips of olive oil, and then she slipped it in, just like that. It wasn't large, just a couple of inches long, but it was wide enough that she enjoyed

153

watching Sam's ringed muscle stretch around it before closing back around the narrow piece. The flared bit kept it from sliding all the way in, and she pressed against it, just to make sure it wasn't going to go anywhere. Sam had been silent during its insertion but he moaned when she pushed it, so she pushed it again and his throat released a most delightful whine. Becky thought about sniffing it, getting down on her knees and rubbing the tip of her nose against it, but she refrained. Maybe later. Maybe when Chad was with them.

"How does it feel?" Becky leaned past him to wash her hands at the sink. He took the moment to stand and pull his underwear and trousers back up. She couldn't help but notice that his dick—half-hard, not as big as Chad's but still thick, and uncut—was surrounded by naked skin that was, like his ass, completely devoid of hair, except for a patch of dark curls just at the base, a few inches below his belly button. It was covered up almost as soon as she'd seen it, but she was positive: Sam waxed, and he had a soul patch for his dick. That was also a bit strange but, again, she wasn't going to complain.

"It tingles," he answered, washing his own hands, "not even a burn. I've heard that it's not as bad if you're into spicy foods, though, like your body's already used to it." He took the paring knife and started on the second piece of ginger. "Do you like spicy things, Becky?"

She started to answer, but before she could get out what she was planning to be a flirtatious *yes*, Sam yelled and the knife clattered in the sink. Becky was ready to laugh, thinking that the ginger was more of a burn than he'd thought at first, but then she saw the blood and realized he'd cut himself.

"Dammit!" He shouted, and turned on the water to wash it off. "It hurts more with the ginger juice."

"That's bleeding hard." Becky pulled a handful of paper towels off the roll and he pulled his hand out of the stream and pressed his fingers into the thick wad. The blood soaked through very quickly, and Sam swore.

"Let me go... no, wait," Becky looked over her shoulder at the open doorway. "CHAD!" She cried out, "CHAD! SAM CUT HIS FINGER, WE NEED THE FIRST AID KIT!"

His voice answered, faintly, "Yeah, I can get it, I'll be right down! Hey Sam!"

Becky smiled back at Sam, who was refolding the towels to a fresh area that he could dirty up as his finger continued to bleed, his face drawn up in annoyance. "We have a good kit, we'll get you patched up."

"I'm so sorry, Becky, I know this isn't fun for you. I gotta admit that this evening has already been more than I was expecting in my wildest dreams and *oh my god, what the fuck is that?*"

Sam wasn't exactly pointing—the mass of paper towels wouldn't allow for it—but he was gesturing wildly towards the kitchen door. Becky figured that it wasn't Chad showing up with the first aid kit. Without even glancing back she answered nonchalantly, "oh, those are just the bugs." She took Sam gently by the elbow and led him to the table, sitting him in a chair and then lowering herself next to him, facing the doorway. Millie was there, and Wings too, and a few beetles, and an ant and... Eddie? The red, angry looking winged thing with the dripping backside sure looked like Eddie, anyway.

"Those are some big fuckin' bugs," Sam murmured as they shuffled into the room, carefully keeping their distance but clearly interested. "Are they your pets or something? I've never seen anything like it."

"Oh, no," Becky shook her head, "not pets. They're wild, I guess? They live behind the basement wall, and they come up to visit sometimes."

"That so?" Sam reached out with his undamaged hand like you would when you're meeting a new dog, but they ignored it, instead focusing on his cut hand. All of them except for Eddie, who sneaked around behind his chair. "They seem interested in the blood." He pulled his hands back and lifted his feet off the ground. "Will they hurt me?"

Becky, trying not to think about Bates, and what Thelma had done to Eddie earlier, shook her head. "No, we've, uh, known them for almost as long as we've lived here. They've never hurt us." It wasn't a lie, anyway.

Chad was announced by heavy footsteps on the stairs, and the bugs all turned to him and chittered a greeting when he hopped into the room.

"Hey, guys!" He said cheerily. "Hey, Sam. You cut yourself?"

"He was carving a butt plug out of ginger and his hand slipped." Sam flushed, and Chad's eyebrows raised in surprise, but they both took her announcement in stride.

"Oh yeah?" Chad asked, as he threw himself into the third chair and opened up the first aid kit. "Who's it for?"

"It was for her," Sam answered, resting his injured hand on the table in front of Chad, "but I'd already made one for myself."

He shifted sideways in his chair and lifted the corner of his mouth into another one of those goddamn cocky smiles, and Becky was tickled to see the tips of Chad's ears redden where they peeked through his damp hair. Chad took a pair of latex gloves out of the kit and proceeded to pull them on. Or he tried to, anyway—judging by the way he was struggling with them, they were a size or two too small.

Conversation ceased as all of them—Sam, Becky, and all the bugs but one—watched Chad try to pull on those little blue gloves. The problem was that he couldn't fit more than three fingers into the glove. He tried wiggling in four fingers and then pulling the rest of the glove over the wider part of his hand, but the glove would just snap back off and land on the table. And even when he could get his fingers in, it was clear that they were really too long for the gloves to fit; the glove fingers ended around his knuckles. It was ridiculous, and Becky was preparing to make a joke, until she looked up and saw the expression on Sam's face.

Sam was into Chad trying to put on those latex gloves. His brown eyes were opened wide, as big as platters, and his pupils were dark. His mouth hung open and his hand lay loose, bleeding freely on the table, and his dick was clearly hard and visible against the front of his trousers. Becky tapped Chad on the shoulder and when Chad looked up he saw it, too. The men gazed at each other for one long, tension filled moment, but when one of the more inquisitive beetles appeared on the table and attempted to take a taste of Sam's blood, Becky decided enough was enough.

"Chad, you just had a shower so your hands should be clean. Why don't you use the hand sanitizer in there and just, you know, raw him? Go in naked?"

The glove that Chad had been trying to pull on snapped off and flew across the room, much to the amusement of the bugs, landing beside the trash can. The men were breathing heavily, and they seemed not to notice. Chad, without a word and without taking his eyes off of Sam, picked up the little bottle of sanitizer and squeezed it into one hand, then rubbed them both together, being careful to massage it down in between each finger.

"I wouldn't want you to get an infection," Chad murmured as he scooted his chair closer and, taking a piece of gauze and the wound wash, proceeded to carefully clean Sam's wound.

Becky stood by the sink, fresh glass of wine in hand, and watched the proceedings with great amusement and not a small amount of excitement. The process of cleaning and bandaging Sam's cut was clearly a kind of foreplay for them, almost a ritual. The washing of the wound was bathing, to ensure the body was clean; the antibacterial ointment was a prophylactic, to ensure no future harm would come; the unwinding of the roll of gauze was the undressing; and the wrapping of the wound was a kind of aftercare.

Okay, it was silly, but Becky was getting tipsy and the looks the guys were giving each other were really turning her on. Sam kept moving around in his seat and she couldn't stop thinking about his sweet, juicy ass, and his dick, which had also looked very juicy although she hadn't gotten a very good look at it. She thought, perhaps, she could get a better, longer, deeper look at it soon. The bugs were getting turned on, too, they could sense what was happening and they'd slowly moved closer, their backsides beginning to drip little trails of fluid across the floor.

In no time at all Sam's hand was all wrapped and the spell was broken. Becky glanced at the clock on the stove.

"Oh no, guys, it's almost seven and we still haven't even started dinner!"

When she glanced back at them, Chad was on his knees, rubbing his cheek against Sam's knee, and Sam's good hand was digging deep into his hair as though he was the best boy in the world and deserved all the pets he could give. Sam looked over at her, a bit guilty.

"Uh... I think we're gonna do something over here, if you don't mind? There's just something about first aid kits that gets me every time."

Becky narrowed her eyes at him. "Sam, did you cut yourself on purpose?"

He didn't answer, but the way he shifted his hips on the chair and the guilty expression that darted across his face told her everything she needed to know. Still, she couldn't bring herself to be too upset about it.

"Okay, then," she said, turning back to the cutting board and the half-sliced red pepper. "You guys do your thing, I just need to slice these up and then it won't take much time at all. The rice is already cooked, so that's easy enough.

Becky smiled to herself as she heard the unmistakable sound of a zipper, followed by a wet *slurp*, a pair of deep moans, and a chitter of admiration. Taking another sip of wine she picked up her knife; she was already looking forward to dessert.

Chapter Twenty-Six

CHAD WAS REALLY GOING to town on Sam, and Sam was appreciative of his endeavors. There had always been something about Chad's mouth—the plush of his lips, the way he moved his jaw—that screamed that he'd be good at oral and Sam was excited to *finally* have an opportunity to see that theory through. He now had proof that Chad was excellent at sucking dick, and since that theory was confirmed his new theory was that he was equally good at licking clit. He held Chad's hair in the fist of his uninjured hand, felt the burning of the ginger in his ass meld with the pleasure growing from Chad's lips, and watched Becky. She was at the counter, her back to them, slicing peppers and chicken breasts, occasionally glancing over her shoulder at them and pressing her thighs together in a way that made it pretty clear that she was turned on. Maybe, Sam thought, he'd get to see Chad eat some pussy later. Maybe, he thought, he would get to eat some pussy too.

The sky's the limit, really.

Several minutes into it, Sam was just thinking he might be ready to give Chad a cum injection in the back of his throat—just to see if he could take it—when a big red bug came out from behind Sam's chair and Chad went a little crazy. He took his mouth off Sam's dick, which was a really unfortunate thing, and shouted joyfully, which was... kind of cute, actually. Chad sat back and started touching that bug, rubbing it on its head and between its wings.

"Eddie!" He shouted. "Eddie! You're okay!"

Sam was confused, to say the least. The pet bugs were interesting—he'd never seen anything like it, for sure. But Becky and Chad were cool with them and Chad was clearly attached to this red one—Eddie, his name was. Eddie, for his part—once he was done being reacquainted with Chad, or whatever it was that was happening—seemed to be very interested in Sam's dick. Sam smiled as the bug examined it, moving in close and waving its little antennae around it.

"Hey, man," he said after a minute, hand fisting his dick to keep it from going soft, "I'm happy for you and your friend, I guess you haven't seen each other in a while and that's great, but..." he gripped Chad's chin with his unoccupied hand and swiveled Chad's head back to face his lap, "your mouth felt so good on my dick, you're such a good boy, my little Chad. I'd like you to keep going. Please."

Sam had learned a thing or two about Chad in the time he'd worked as his supervisor, and the main thing he'd learned is that the man thrived on praise. If you needed Chad to get work done all you had to do was tell him he was *good*, how valuable he was, smart and hard working yes, but the word *good* always made him stand up straighter, work just a bit faster. As with Chad's mouth, Sam had sometimes wondered if his theories about Chad's attachment to praise extended to other realms, outside of work. As with his mouth, it appeared Sam's theories were correct.

Sam glanced over at Becky again. She was leaning against the sink, wine glass in hand, chicken all but forgotten behind her. She watched as her boyfriend gave Eddie one last scratch, then sat back up on his knees and took Sam's dick between his lips. He hummed, and the vibration went straight to Sam's balls.

"Oh yeah, baby. Take Daddy's meat like a good boy, oh yeah."

Sam heard Becky cough into her wine glass and he could guess why, but when he'd said *Daddy's meat* Chad had groaned and sucked harder, so he didn't care too much about what Becky thought just at that moment.

"Yeah, baby. Suck that dick. Suck it hard enough and Daddy's gonna come right in your throat."

Apparently baby Chad wanted that cum in his throat, because he sucked so hard Sam felt like his balls were going to go into his vas deferens and all the way through. Luckily it wasn't quite hard enough to do that, but Sam could tell it was just a truly impressive amount of cum. Chad took it though, and swallowed it down, and the bugs—there were more of them now, Sam was sure of it, they carpeted the floor of the kitchen and into the hallway—made noise like they were cheering. It was the best audience Sam'd had for a while, and he couldn't help but acknowledge them with a nod of his head and a wink.

Sam was prepared to keep going, in any possible direction, but Chad declared that he was hungry for food.

"Your cum tastes good," Chad said to Sam a minute later, as he took up a knife to finish up the second ginger plug, "but I'm a big man and I need more than even you can give me." Sam wanted to argue but he knew that Chad was probably right, and he congratulated himself

162

for his preemptive pineapple juice drinking as he sat at the table and watched the other two cook.

He petted the bugs while he waited. They did seem to be very interested in him, particularly in the parts of him that resided above his knees and below his waist. Eddie, the red one, kept sniffing at his butt, and his belly did something unexpected when a long trail of viscous liquid dripped out of the thing's backside and landed on the floor with a *plop*.

"That's, ah," he said to Chad as he set a plate of Thai curry in front of him. "That is, your giant bug is making a bit of a mess."

"Yeah, he'll do that." Chad answered, sitting down with his own plate and pouring more wine for both of them.

"It means he wants to fuck." Becky added, taking her own seat.

Sam choked on his first bite—it was delicious, spicy and heavy with the flavor of ginger—and the other two waited patiently until he'd stopped coughing.

"Excuse me? I think I misheard you. What did you say?"

"I said," Becky spoke slowly, her consonants crisp, "that Eddie wants to fuck."

"Eddie pretty much always wants to fuck," Chad added with a shrug. "It's a thing with him."

"Ah," Sam said, turning over various ideas in his head. "Ah. You mean, like, the other bugs?"

Another shrug from Chad. "He's not picky. Bugs, ass, pussy. Once I was doing some rewiring and he tried to fuck the hole in the wall, he almost got electrocuted. Stupid horny bug."

Sam finished his glass of wine in two gulps and Becky refilled it.

"Did you say *ass* and *pussy*?"

Becky leveled him a patient smile. "We're low key telling you we fuck the giant bugs."

"Ah."

"And we're also telling you that Eddie will fuck you, if you want him to."

"He's a good fuck," Chad mumbled through a mouthful of curry and rice. "Knows what he's doing, exactly what you need." He paused to swallow.

"I don't know, man, I usually top. Could I top one of them?"

Becky and Chad traded a glance. "Not really," Becky answered, "but Millie could suck your dick."

Sam ate his curry and considered his options. Even putting aside whatever something called *Millie* might be he'd already had his dick sucked, and he really wanted something else. He'd walked in the door wanting to fuck Becky, or maybe Chad, and the blowjob had seemed like a sweet (though not *wholly* unexpected) bonus. Getting fucked in the ass by a giant red winged thing with lube dripping out of its butt hadn't even been on his radar, and he just needed a moment to think.

But while he was thinking—drinking his wine and eating his food and making small talk while the giant bugs swarmed around their feet—another one showed up, and suddenly Sam was able to make up his mind.

"*I'm in heaven*," he breathed as the gorgeous vision in green scrambled noisily through the door. "Who the fuck is *that*?"

Chad glanced over his shoulder and traded a look with Becky that Sam couldn't have deciphered even if he'd seen it.

"That's Thelma," said Chad.

"Does Thelma, uh, fuck?"

164

Becky coughed into her glass again.

"She does fuck," Chad replied. "She really does."

An hour later, Sam found out just exactly how she fucked. They'd finished eating. He was full, but not so full that it would slow him down, and he was confident that it would take an hour or two for the spice to work its way through his system so he wasn't too concerned on that end of things. They each poured another glass of wine and relocated to the living room. His ginger plug had lost its bite but when he said something about going to the bathroom to extract it, Chad had insisted that they all just get undressed and he could do it right there in the living room, and then they could get started.

It was a bit strange, taking off his clothes in the living room carpeted with giant bugs, alongside his former employee and his former employee's girlfriend, both of whom he'd been interested in for almost as long as he could remember. Chad, with his large body and soft manner, and Becky, so sharp but also sweet. They were complementary, undoubtedly a good couple, and Sam had thought many times about what it would be like to get between them, physically speaking.

Now that it was happening he wasn't sure anymore what he wanted. The one they called Thelma—the tall one with the long body and long limbs and bulging eyes—she was really something. And she was looking at Sam and the tip of her was dripping in a way that implied that she was thinking exactly the same thing he was.

Becky finished undressing first, and when she threw her underwear to the ground—where, Sam couldn't help but notice, it was grabbed by one of the smaller black beetles who quickly ran away with it—she set her fists on her hips and declared, "I haven't been spit-roasted in forever. Can we do that? Since Sam's already had his dick sucked he can fuck me, and Chad, I'll take your dick." She glanced over at Thelma, who was wobbling slightly a few feet away and creating a slowly-growing puddle on the floor beneath her. "It looks like Thelma wants in, too. Sam, can you take her? And Chad, you can take Eddie, too." Sam hadn't noticed Eddie, but he saw him now, lurking in the shadows just behind Chad. He appeared to be vibrating, and was dripping a little puddle of his own, shiny on the hardwood.

Both men asserted their consent, and Becky was off again. Sam took the opportunity to check out Chad. He looked pretty much exactly as Sam had anticipated. He was muscular and thick but not overly built, like a weightlifter or anything. His dick wasn't completely hard, it hung long and thick and the sight of it made Sam's mouth water. He was going to get to see that dick in Becky's mouth, up close and personal, and it was going to be beautiful. He wanted to know what Chad would look like when he was teased and pushed and finally taken over the edge. It was going to be glorious, he was sure of it.

Chad, for his part, was eyeing Sam in much the same way. His eyes lingered on Sam's dick. Sam knew it wasn't the biggest, it certainly wasn't as big as Chad's, but he had it manscaped nicely and, however it might look, he knew how to use it. He'd use it on Becky in a minute, and then Chad would see., He would know. Once Chad was finished gaping he pulled the coffee table away from the front of the sofa, shooing the gathered bugs away as he did it, and then he pulled the cushions off the sofa and laid them out on the ground before grabbing the knit blanket off the back of the sofa—it looked soft and comfy, and like it had been knitted by someone's grandmother—and draped it over the cushions.

"We'll do it here," he said, as he straightened the blanket out. "Does that work for you?"

"Sure, man, looks good to me." There was something primal about having a little orgy on the floor of the living room, and Sam was totally into it.

Becky came back with a box of condoms, a towel, a small bottle of lube, and the ginger plug that Chad had finished up before dinner. She handed the towel to Chad, who laid it on one end of the cushions, and handed the condoms to Sam.

"One for you, and for Thelma if you want. We go bareback with the bugs but I can understand if you find that unnerving." The smile she gave him was friendly enough but also contained a challenge, and if there's one thing Sam enjoyed it was meeting a challenge and punching it in the face.

"Just for me, I think," he replied, separating off one of the condoms from the strip and making a production of rolling it onto his erection. "I can take her."

Becky's smile sharpened. "I bet you can."

He just grinned, and watched as she laid back on the cushions, butt on the towel, plug and lube in hand. The bugs gathered closely around, they'd even climbed up on the sofa—a green one that reminded Sam very much of Eddie took a position of prominence in the middle of the back of the sofa, a high perch from which it would be able to see everything. Becky pulled her knees up, exposing herself to everyone. Her pussy was beautiful. A bit fuzzy, not smoothly shaven but very finely trimmed, and her pussy lips were clearly visible, pink and dewy and swollen, as though she'd been on the edge of excitement for quite a while. Her asshole was a dusky brown and as he watched it she clenched it, the muscle turning very slightly in on itself.

"Fuck," Sam murmured, and Becky took one lubed-up digit and pressed against it.

"We still have this plug," she said, holding it up in her other hand, "and it seems a shame to waste it. Help?"

She didn't have to ask twice. Sam took the plug between his fingers—she'd already coated it with lube—and pushed it into her waiting hole. The ring of muscle expanded when he pushed the large end through, and then closed around the crudely-crafted base.

"Fuck," he murmured again, echoed by Chad. Eddie had already climbed onto Chad, and appeared to be dividing his attention between teasing Chad's asshole with the tip of his... whatever the body of an insect was called—thorax? Abdomen?—and watching what Sam was doing to Becky. She wiggled her backside and moaned; Sam placed his hands on her thighs and pushed down, holding her tight, to keep her from moving. She moaned again, more like a whimper, and Sam chuckled to himself. "Yeah, you like that, don't you," he whispered, gazing up at her from under his eyelashes. "You like it when Daddy holds you tight." The bugs chittered quietly, and Sam took that as a good sign.

He expected Becky to laugh, the way she did when he was daddy-talking Chad in the kitchen earlier, but to his surprise and delight she bit her lip, whined again, and then murmured, "Oh, Daddy, it's so *hot*."

Whether she was talking about the spice of the plug or him holding her down Sam wasn't sure, but he didn't really care and from the state of his dick—now standing fully at attention where he kneeled next to Becky's head—Chad didn't care either. Without taking his eyes off Becky's face Sam reached out with his thumbs and swept the right one across her opening and up to press on her clit, and the other he set against the base of the plug that peeked out of her asshole and pressed. She shuddered and made a valiant attempt to thrust her hips up, but he continued to hold her down.

"Come on now, be a good girl," he tutted, beginning a slow rotation around her clit. "Chad's dick is right there, why don't you give it a lick?"

She did one better than that—she took the tip of Chad's dick between her lips and sucked it down her throat like it was a cool vanilla milkshake on the hottest day of summer, and she was both starving and suffering from heat stroke. Chad yelped and fell forward, catching himself on the edge of the sofa. The bugs there trilled sympathetically. Sam chuckled and took a moment to check the status of his condom—he probably should have waited to put it on, too late now—but he was still quite hard and it wasn't slipping, so he scooted back and gave Becky's pussy a kiss.

It was divine. She tasted just slightly sweet, a bit like honeysuckle—he smiled against her at the thought—but more earthy. He opened the kiss and dipped his tongue into her opening, then swiped his tongue up to finish with his lips around her clit. He suckled it tenderly, and kept his left thumb solid on the base of the plug, rotating it slowly and gently inside her.

In the meantime Chad started making more noise. Sam ventured a glance up to find that Eddie had breached Chad's ass, and was apparently having a grand time pounding him while Becky still had his dick down her throat on the other side. Chad's mouth was open and his eyes were closed, and he looked like he was having a fine time indeed. The bugs were clearly into it as well, the tension in the air was palpable and there was a lot of dripping going on. Sam wondered vaguely how much his friends spent on upholstery cleaning. For her part Becky hadn't stopped moaning, although her expression had started to take on a note of frustration.

Good.

As Sam brought his attention back to her soft, sweet pussy and sucked on her inner lips, something scratched his back. That's right—Thelma. He hadn't forgotten about her, no he hadn't. He sucked and licked Becky's pussy while the creature climbed on, wrapped her front legs around his shoulders, and chirped with a voice that was surprisingly smooth and deep.

"Hey, little girl," he murmured to Becky before giving her clit another suck, and grinned at her responding shudder and her cry, which was dampened by the fact that Chad's dick was at that time pressing against the back of her throat. She pulled her mouth off with a *pop*.

"Goddammit, Sam," she muttered, "get up here and fuck me already, I want to come on your dick, not your mouth, and I'm already so close."

"That's what I've been waiting to hear, little girl," he answered, crawling up her body carefully so as not to dislodge the giant bug on his back. "Daddy's gonna give you what you need, don't worry."

"I'm not *worried*," she insisted, tugging on Chad's dick and preparing to slip it back into her mouth. "I know you'll take care of me, *Daddy*. I'm just getting tired of waiting for it."

Becky was being a brat, but Sam didn't mind too much. He was going to make her come so hard she sees stars, and then they'd see how bratty she would be.

Three things happened at once. Sam, who'd finished his slow climb up Becky's body, finally pressed his dick into her warm, wet hole. Becky took Chad's dick back into her throat; she hummed happily, and Chad answered with a whine. That bug was really going to town on his ass; Sam was both impressed, and a little bit concerned, given that he had his own bug to deal with. A bug named Thelma, who was in the process of easing her own body into his willing asshole.

It was a strange sensation. Sam wasn't used to taking it anyway, he wasn't lying when he said he usually tops. He'd worn butt plugs, sure, and been pegged a couple of times (his brief fling with the CEO of the company had been illuminating in many ways, including that) but despite his earlier joke about Bates, Sam had only ever topped in their relationship. Poor Bates, he'd been an asshole but he'd been an excellent fuck, and even now Sam missed his pasty grimace. He wondered where he'd gone, and what he would have thought about fucking giant, monstrous, sentient bugs.

Thelma's backend was very narrow but widened quickly, so it didn't hit deep but it gave him a good stretch and she was somehow able to angle it so it rubbed right up against his prostate with each thrust. The liquid that had puddled around her earlier—he was trying not to think too hard about what exactly it was—turned out to be excellent lubrication, and he could feel it, slick and warm, slipping out of his ass and down his thighs. She fucked hard, but also sweetly, and her front limbs were long and strong and wrapped around his chest. She nibbled the back of his neck, too, and that felt pretty good.

"Yeah, Mama," he murmured as she thrusted and bit and clutched him around the shoulders. "Good Mama, make your boy feel good, yeah."

Thelma behind him, Becky on his dick, Chad's dick in Becky's face just inches from his own... it was pretty close to heaven. The insectoid audience seemed to be getting off on it too, there was a lot of noise, squeaks and trills and vibrating wings and also, he could see now, other things—worms and other long things that had legs—writhing around on the floor in a way that reminded him of the time a girl he'd been trying to get with invited him to her church and it turned out she was a Pentecostal.

Everybody was making their own noises, and Sam thought it was only polite to check in and see how Becky was holding up.

"How you doing, little girl," he murmured, his hips smacking wetly against her thighs, the tempo matching the speed at which Thelma was reaming his ass. "Are you getting close? You gonna come hard on Daddy's dick?"

She pulled her mouth off Chad's dick—another satisfying, wet *pop*, which Chad reacted to with a whine—and spittle spattered on her chin. Chad's face was a shiny red and his eyes were dark and wide, and Eddie was still pounding into him, now whining steadily on a high, eerie tone; Chad looked like he was ready to break any minute.

Chad glanced down at Sam and an expression of concern pushed out some of the lust from his face. "Hey man, is she hurting you?" He gestured behind Sam—Sam assumed at the giant bug who was fucking him and still nibbling his neck. "You okay with that?"

"Fuckin' good," Sam responded. "You weren't kidding when you said these bugs know how to fuck."

Chad nodded, still looking concerned, and Becky finally had a chance to catch her breath to answer Sam's question.

"S'good," she responded breathily, "m'close. Just need a little more, just a bit more." As he watched she reached out her right hand and three of the little worms he'd noticed earlier crawled over and into her hand. She dumped them onto her stomach, and the two larger ones crawled up and attached themselves to her nipples while the smaller one crawled down, between their bodies, and latched onto her clit.

"Oh, *yeah*," she whined loudly, "those little worms suck me *so good!*"

"Holy shit." Sam didn't think that there was anything else that could happen to surprise him, but he'd been wrong. "Holy shit." He looked down between their bodies to glimpse the little worm on her clit, wiggling happily. He set himself just a tad more upright, to avoid crushing it. He expected everybody would be mad at him if that happened, and he didn't want to consider what the punishment for that might be.

Becky gritted her teeth and stared at him with shining eyes. Her hand was tugging on Chad's dick like it was a water pump and she was in danger of dying of thirst. "Sam, I'm gonna come, but I need one more thing. Please?" Becky was the picture of lust, and who was he to say no?

"Anything, little girl. What do you need?"

"Put your hand around my throat, Daddy." Her voice was quiet and strained, and its sound combined with her unexpected request almost had him coming then and there. "I'm gonna come and if you do that it's gonna be *so hard*, please, I wanna come hard while you choke me, please Daddy."

173

The chittering of the bugs got a little bit louder, and Chad swore as Becky took his dick back into her mouth, her eyes pleading up at Sam. Thelma was really working his prostate now, and Sam could tell that Eddie was working Chad's, so really there was only one thing left to do. He reached out and carefully placed his right hand around Becky's throat. He squeezed, not hard, but with enough force to cut off her breathing.

Her chest stopped moving and she seized up immediately, her pussy fluttering violently around Sam's dick. Thelma's ... not teeth. Beak? Mouth? Whatever, it was hard and it sucked and it scraped with almost brutal force around Sam's neck. He was going to have quite the hickey tomorrow. Chad shouted and threw himself backwards, the movement wrenching his dick out of Becky's mouth and spraying cum everywhere, to the obvious delight of the bugs. Somewhere in there Sam became aware of his own orgasm, harsh and huge and glorious, and he shouted his own victory and lifted his hand from around Becky's throat. She took in a deep breath and just kept coming. Sam worked her through it, still hard even though he'd already come, and eventually her legs stopped quivering and he was able to pull out.

He turned around to find that Thelma had pulled out and deposited a shiny clutch of eggs all over the floor behind him, and he heard Eddie do something similar behind Chad. That explained all the liquid, anyway. Sam tried not to think about it too hard. When he had time to think about it later, he decided it had been worth it.

Thirty minutes later they'd all cleaned up and thrown away the ginger and the bugs had said goodnight and returned to their home behind the wall in the basement, taking Becky's underwear with them because, Sam supposed, they were just like that. (He would have taken Becky's underwear, too, if he thought he could get away with it.) The three humans were drinking beers in the living room, the coffee table and blanket returned to their rightful places.

"So," Sam said from the armchair, after a few moments of silence, "that was interesting. You do that all the time?"

Becky, bare feet tucked under her butt, leaned against Chad and looked thoughtful.

"I mean," she said, "not *all* the time."

"Maybe a few nights a week," Chad added, "and usually it's just us and one or two of the bugs, up in the bedroom. This is kind of a special occasion."

"This is more like when Chad's brother comes to visit."

"Yeah, that's right. This is like, once in a blue moon." Chad took a sip of his beer. "Was it fun?"

"Fuck, yeah. It was a lot of fun. I do have one question for you, though."

They looked at him expectantly over the necks of their beer bottles.

"How much do you spend on upholstery cleaning?"

They both nodded sagely.

"Yes, that's a big issue, obviously," Chad answered. "We used to rent a thing from Home Depot, but after the third time we just bought our own."

"A Bissell Spot Clean Pet Pro," Becky continued. "It's great! We mostly try to cover things now, but sometimes it's easier to let the mess happen and then clean up after."

Sam supposed that was a pretty good approach.

They had a couple more beers before they said their goodnights. Sam promised to find an excuse to come back to town, and they promised that if he did they'd arrange another orgy with the bugs. It had been a strange experience, but definitely something he wanted to do again.

As he bid them adieu at the door, Sam leaned into Becky and whispered, "give Daddy a goodnight kiss, little girl." She smacked him instead, but it was good natured, and then she hugged him, so he supposed it was okay after all.

Chapter Twenty-Seven

CHAD HAD A NEW routine, and it was a secret.

Every evening, after dinner, Chad would give Becky a kiss as she loaded the dishwasher, and then he would head upstairs to the guest bedroom. That room was on the other side of the staircase from the bedroom they shared, and it was smaller—just large enough for a queen-sized bed and a floating desk on the interior wall behind the door. The room didn't get used much, unless Brock or Earl were visiting from out of town, but it was handy if either Becky or Chad needed to be someplace quiet, or private, or just to have some time to themselves.

Chad had a good excuse, because he really did have a lot of work, and he had to bring some of it home with him. That wasn't a lie. The company had finally replaced Bates, but they were still trying to hire someone to replace Chad, who had moved into Sam's manager position after he'd left. This meant that Chad still had project work on top of managing everybody else. A couple of hours of work at home at night was a pain, but it was an excellent excuse to sit by himself.

Well, not completely by himself; this was the secret part. After kissing Becky and treading up the stairs, he would settle himself at the desk, open the laptop, and take off his shirt. Usually by that time the worms had crawled up from the corner where they had taken to waiting for him. He would say hello, give them little pats on each of their little heads, and lift them up so they could latch onto his nipples.

Chad was determined to make himself lactate, and the worms were going to help him.

He hadn't come up with the idea on his own. He and Becky had been at the dentist together, for their regular six-month cleaning appointments, and his hygienist had been running just a bit later than Becky's. So once she'd gone in to start her cleaning, he got bored and dug through the magazine bin for something to read. He'd happened upon an old issue of Scientific American, which had opened directly to an article about male lactation.

Chad was intrigued. He'd never thought about lactation—he never even thought about Becky lactating—but as he read the article he started turning the idea over in his head. It would be neat to train his body to make milk. It might feel good. And Becky, he was sure, would love it. She was pretty kinky, it turned out—the giant, horny bugs in their basement had been teaching them all sorts of new things, and Chad guessed that getting milk out of his chest would appeal to them, too. They loved messes, and cleaning them up. If Chad could really start producing, he could make a righteous mess. The more he thought about it, the more certain he was that he wanted to do it.

Eventually he had to go in for his cleaning, and of course he had to leave the magazine, but once he got home he started searching for information on how to make it happen. There were prescription drugs, but he certainly wasn't going to go visit kind old Dr Armstrong and ask for a script, no way. So he went the natural route instead, and popped onto Amazon to order up More Milk Plus, liquid fenugreek, and lactation tea (all delivered to his work in plain wrappers, naturally). He took extra dosages of all of it, and arranged with the worms for them to meet him in the guest bedroom at night and suck on his nipples for a couple of hours. It tired them out pretty quickly so they had to work in shifts, and sometimes a few of the other bugs would show up to watch. Chad didn't mind, especially the first night that Wings showed up and got so excited it ended up fucking Chad on the floor while the worms did their work. It had been amazing, although they'd had to stay very quiet so Becky wouldn't figure out what was going on.

It took a month of supplements and nightly worm sucking (and, by the end, Chad was getting fucked almost every night) but it finally worked—Chad's breasts were producing milk.

He could feel it when it finally happened. Something was definitely different, had been growing during the day, a fullness in his chest that hadn't been there the day before. When the worms latched on there was a definite tingle, a new sensation, and when they started sucking he could feel the milk moving out of him and into them.

The worms, both of them, dropped right off and onto the laptop keyboard. They wiggled around and squeaked at each other, and the other bugs in the room—Eddie and Wings both that night—trilled quietly and shook their wings in celebration. Chad didn't know if they had understood what exactly he was trying to do, but they seemed pleased by it.

Chad got fucked twice that night, and Eddie and Wings both sampled the milk.

Chad was pleased, but he wanted to be producing more milk before he showed Becky, so the nightly visits continued. For another week, Chad hosted rotating pairs of worms on his chest, and more and more of the other creatures came to watch. It was tiring, but it was worth it. Eventually he was so full he was in pain by the time dinner was over—by this time Becky was noticing that something was up, so he decided it was definitely time to let her in on his surprise.

That Friday, after dinner, instead of taking his laptop upstairs, he sat down with Becky in the living room.

He was nervous.

"Sweetheart, I have a surprise for you."

She bit her lip and smiled up at him.

"That's fun, I love surprises! And as it happens, I have a surprise for you, too."

"Oh! Would you like to give me your surprise first, or would you like to get yours?"

Becky hummed. "Maybe it would be better for you to give me mine first. Mine's a little... involved."

Chad nodded, wondering a bit what her surprise for him might be and also worried that she wouldn't like his after all. Only one way to find out.

"Okay. I have to take my shirt off first."

"What a coincidence...!" She threw her head back and laughed. "I have to take mine off, too. Why don't we do it together?"

Chad readily agreed, and they both took their shirts off. As Chad watched Becky remove her bra, he was certain that her breasts looked a bit bigger than he remembered them. How long had it been since he'd seen them, anyway? Too long. He'd been wearing himself out every night for the last month catching up on work, lactation training, and fucking the bugs, and Becky hadn't asked him for sex in that time. Which seemed... a bit strange, actually, now that he thought about it. But anyway, yes, her breasts were definitely larger; swollen, even. And her nipples were very pink. Her nipples looked *amazing*, ripe and ready for sucking, and Chad desperately wanted them in his mouth.

At the same time, his own breasts were feeling very full, and the telltale tingle was getting stronger by the second. He needed to be sucked on, too. As he thought about it—about Becky, lowering her head to his chest and sucking on his nipple, while she plucked the other between her fingers, and then switched—he felt a drip of liquid splash down onto his belly.

Becky gasped. "*Chad*. Is that *milk*?" Her voice was breathy, which seemed like a good sign, and when he looked up at her he could see her eyes, wide, staring at his chest, where a drip of white fluid was preparing to fall from the tip of his other nipple. Her cheeks were red, a flush that traveled down her neck and to her chest.

Chad couldn't help but notice that her nipples were dripping, too.

"Becky," he murmured, hardly believing it. "Becky. You have milk, too."

"Yeah, there was an article at the dentist's office, and it got me thinking..."

"Me too. I wanted to surprise you, so I did some research..."

"And ordered the herbal supplements and the tea..."

"And every night when I work upstairs the worms come and suck my nipples..."

"And sometimes the others come, too..."

"And we fuck..."

"And that's why we haven't had sex in a month." Becky finished with a giggle.

Chad scooted closer to her on the sofa. "We can make up for it now." He lifted a hand up and cradled her left breast. It was definitely heavier than it had been the last time he'd held it like that. He squeezed it gently, and several drops of milk flowed out and onto his hand. It was warm, and smelled sweet, and he wanted to taste it. So he did. He lowered his face to her breast, took her nipple between his lips, swirled his tongue around its hardened peak, and gently started to suck.

Becky moaned and grabbed his head with both her hands, clasping his hair in her fists.

"Oh *Chad* ," she whined. "Oh my god, that feels so good. I've felt so *full* ... All I could think about was what it would feel like for you to suck the milk out of my tits.

Chad hummed but didn't say anything—his mouth was full of her warm, sweet milk, and the harder he sucked the more milk he got. He switched his attention to her other breast, which had been dripping steadily, creating a little stream of milk down her front that was pooling at the waistband of her shorts. That seemed like a waste to him, so he helped her pull her shorts and underwear down and off—to the chittering cheers of a group of bugs that had been quietly gathering over the past few minutes. With her underwear off he could smell her pussy, and he wanted to suck on it, but the stream of milk was calling him, too. He was torn, but only until one of the beetles and an ant stepped forward and volunteered to help out in that regard, so Chad could concentrate on her breasts.

"Thank you," he said politely, as they got to work on Becky's pussy, and he licked the stream of milk from Becky's belly all the way up to her nipple, which he popped into his mouth and suckled again.

"Fuck, Becky," Chad moaned, popping his lips off her nipple for a moment. She whined as the air chilled her wet skin and struggled to push his face back down. "Your milk is so warm and sweet, it tastes wonderful."

Chad returned to sucking, moving back and forth between her breasts every few minutes, and he was shocked that as much as he was sucking out, the milk just kept coming. Becky was clearly into it, too, she moaned and writhed and mewled while Chad suckled and sucked, and the ant and beetle took turns pleasuring her—just enough that it wasn't quite enough, exactly the way that she insisted she didn't like, but Chad knew she secretly did.

Sucking the milk from Becky's tits was doing something to his own tits—it was making them drip more. But he wasn't about to stop to clean himself up because he didn't want to take his mouth off of Becky. So he sucked, and dripped, and Becky clutched his head to her chest and whined and writhed on the sofa, and the ant and beetle made themselves comfortable between her legs, and the gathering of giant bugs grew. There was a small crowd of them—primed, tense, ready—when Becky finally screamed with the arrival of her orgasm, and milk sprayed from both of her nipples like Old Faithful times two.

The milk gushed into Chad's mouth so violently he choked, and spilled half his mouthful down his front. The bugs closest to him—a group of moths with one incongruous ladybug among them—took that as a clue, and gathered around to lick it off of him. The milk from her other breast rained down on Chad and the bugs nearby, including

183

Wings, who had been perched on the back of the sofa although Chad wasn't sure how long it'd been there. Wings lost it, and let loose a clutch of eggs right there, creating a milky, eggy mess on the back of the sofa.

It was pretty much exactly what Chad had anticipated, five weeks before, as he'd contemplated the article in the old *Scientific American* in the dentist's office, only he was the one who was doing the sucking. But it was perfect.

Becky finally stopped yelling, and her tits stopped gushing, and her legs stopped twitching. The ant and beetle climbed down, and Chad was able to help her sit up and check in on her while Wings and a few others cleaned up the eggs behind her.

"How was that, sweetheart? Was that good?"

She rolled her eyes. "Of course, my god, that was fucking amazing. Was it good for you?"

"So good, Becky. You taste amazing."

She preened and eyed his chest, where his nipples were still dripping little streams of milk down his torso, despite the cleaning from the moths (and ladybug) just a minute earlier. "You look like your tits need sucking, too... we need to do something about that. I can't wait to find out what *you* taste like."

The thought of her mouth on his nipples made them tingle and leak even more, and also made his jeans feel a whole lot tighter.

"Sure thing, but first," he stood up and pulled down his jeans and underwear and kicked them aside. "Only fair that I'm naked, too," he grinned at her and sat back down. Millie suddenly appeared out of the crowd, but Chad waved her away. "Not tonight, Mil, Becky and I haven't fucked each other in a month and I want her to have me all

184

to herself right now." He glanced up at his girlfriend. "If that's alright with you?"

Becky pretended to think, then shrugged and climbed into his lap. She rubbed her heavy, warm breasts against his, mingling the sticky remnants of her breastmilk with the fresh liquid still dripping from his nipples.

"I think that's quite all right," she growled, lowering slowly to impale herself on his dick. It had been so long since Chad's dick had been inside anything other than Millie's maw, he'd almost forgotten how wonderful Becky's slick heat felt when it squeezed around him.

"Fuck *me*," he murmured, and she rotated her hips and lifted up, almost all the way up, before pressing herself down again with an adorable grunt.

"My pleasure," she answered, doing it again, and then one more time before she pushed him to lean against the back of the sofa and lowered her mouth to glide her tongue roughly over his right nipple.

The sensation of her tongue was exquisite, like scratching an itch but the itch only grows stronger. She licked him a second time, and he could feel his body expelling the milk in response to her encouragement. She kept riding him, too, every stroke a bit stronger, a bit faster. Then her lips were around his nipple and she was suckling, humming as she drank down his milk. It leaked out of the corner of her mouth and dripped down her chin, and he could see how her throat bobbed with each swallow and it was the sexiest fucking thing he'd ever seen in his life.

The bugs thought it was sexy too. They were being good, they weren't touching, but they were close, and the air was heavy with their vibrations. She milked his tits with her mouth and she milked his dick with her pussy, and when she finally moved her mouth to his left nipple his body decided it was time to let go. He grabbed her hips and came into her with a roar, thrusting into her over and over as his milk sprayed over her and the sofa and the bugs around them. The combination of the violent letdown with his orgasm reminded Chad of how it had felt to come with the spiders' eggs in his dick, and that made him come even harder. The bugs cheered, and Becky laughed as Chad held her close and rolled onto his back.

"You make the best milk," he said, taking a lick from the sticky sweetness that covered her chest.

"I love yours too," she answered. "It's so sweet and thick. Like your dick and what comes out of it." She giggled and snuggled down. "That was a good surprise."

"A very good surprise," Chad agreed.

Becky was quiet for a moment and Chad listened to the bugs file out. Once the room was quiet, Becky whispered, "maybe tomorrow night we can have milkshakes for dessert."

Chad thought that was an excellent idea.

Epilogue

IN THE DAYS, MONTHS, years, and decades that followed, things continued much in the same way, in the little house built into the side of the mountain. Chad and Becky joyfully fucked and sucked with their buggy friends, and their friends drew on their sexual energy to empower themselves.

But it was all good.

The bugs never took more than was offered, and Chad and Becky never gave more than they safely could—although there were times they really stepped up to the edge of the cliff, so to speak.

Those are stories for another day.

Becky and Chad lived long and happy lives, and they kept going for as long as they could. They sure did! And when they died (because, unlike Eddie, all humans must die) the bugs took their bodies into the mountain and laid them to rest. They would never be alone, and the bugs would never be without them.

FIN

Thanks

I wrote the first stories in what I was then calling the Entomological Pursuits series in 2019. I was drowning in vampire and werewolf erotica and I wanted to read a different kind of monsterfucking. Something that stressed the inhuman monster. And what's more inhuman than bugs? Thank goodness that I had my friend Lindsey there to cheer me on. Her reaction to the first stories encouraged me to continue writing them—on my deathbed I will remember reading to her out loud in her kitchen, while our families hung out just on the other side of the door. How she laughed until she cried when she was supposed to be cooking dinner. I am also thankful to Elena for providing me a list of kinks early on, which gave me fresh ideas for every chapter. I never did finish up that list (sorry, impact play, I'm ashamed I wrote 50k of this and didn't include you) but maybe, someday?

Fast forwarding to 2023, thank you to Cassandra Daucus for encouraging me to pull these out and polish them up. She convinced me that there's an audience for bugs. I hope she's right! I also need to acknowledge the artistic talents of Ruth Anna Evans for designing the beautiful and very bright cover, and Cat Voleur for the formatting and proofreading, and for sending me encouraging notes as she read through it.

Finally, thank you for reading the Acknowledgments! And for reading Becky and Chad and the Bugs in the Basement. I hope you had fun reading about their erotic entomological adventures.

Also By Millie M.

"The Dixorcist" and "SUNDAY SUNDAY SUNDAY" in Cult of Horrotica, Issue 1, October 2023.

Paraesthesia: Three Dark Stories of Nonconsent
The Confessional

Find books by Millie M. on Smashwords: https://www.smashwords.com/profile/view/milliemenagerie